The Experiment

BOOK 2

Formerly titled *Journeys to Fayrah*

The Experiment

LEOLA LIBRARY
LEOLA, PA

Bill Myers

TOMMY NELSON
FOR TWEENS AND TEENS

A Division of Thomas Nelson Publishers
Since 1798

www.thomasnelson.com

Book Two: The Experiment
Copyright © 1991 by Bill Myers
Formerly Titled Journeys to Fayrah

Published in Nashville, Tennessee, by Tommy Nelson®, a Division of Thomas
Nelson, Inc. Visit us on the Web at www.tommynelson.com.

Scripture quotations are from the *International Children's Bible*®, *New Century
Version*®, copyright © 1986, 1988, 1999 by Tommy Nelson®, a Division of
Thomas Nelson, Inc.

Tommy Nelson® books may be purchased in bulk for educational, business,
fund-raising, or sales promotional use. For information, please e-mail us at
SpecialMarkets@ThomasNelson.com.

This is a work of fiction. Names, characters, places, and incidents either are the
product of the author's imagination or are used fictitiously.

Book design: Mark & Jennifer Ross / MJ Ross Design

ISBN 1-4003-0745-7

Printed in the United States of America
05 06 07 08 09 WRZ 9 8 7 6 5 4 3 2 1

For Mackenzie,
Our newest joy and my officemate
throughout this journey

Book 2
The Experiment

CONTENTS

Book 2
The Experiment

Chapter One

Another Day, Another Full Moon

"I have not forgotten!" the harsh voice cawed. "You belong to me. I have not forgotten!"

For the hundredth time, Denise looked up through the gnarled and twisted branches of the frozen forest. And for the hundredth time, she saw the black leather-winged creature circling high overhead. Half woman, half who-knows-what, the animal was enough to give anybody the creeps . . . even if that anybody knew they were only dreaming.

It had been exactly two months since Denise had traveled to Fayrah and had seen the creature. And for two months the ugly thing kept coming back and haunting her in her dreams.

"Surely you've not forgotten?" the voice demanded.

Denise swallowed hard. It took a moment to gather her courage before she finally found her voice. "What do you want from me?" she cried. "Leave me alone!"

Suddenly the entire forest broke into laughter. And more suddenly still Denise realized that she wasn't standing in a forest. Instead, she was sitting in her classroom.

"All I want from you, young lady, is to tell me the subject of this sentence." It was Mrs. Barnick, her English teacher. She stood three desks ahead of Denise with anything but a pleased look on her face.

"Ahhh . . ." Denise stalled, desperately trying to push the dream out of her mind while she searched for the sentence. *What sentence? Where was it? On the blackboard? In my book?* There were more giggles and whispers from those around her. She could feel the tops of her ears start to burn like they always did when she got mad or embarrassed.

"Denny," Mrs. Barnick spoke evenly as she pointed to the side board. "It is sentence number three, from yesterday's assignment: 'The clown's humor was quite bizarre.' "

Denise peered at the board.

"What is the subject of that sentence?" Mrs. Barnick persisted. "What is *bizarre*?"

"She is," a blond-haired kid cracked from two rows over.

Again the room broke into laughter.

The kid grinned proudly over his sharp wit—until his eyes met Denise's—until her look made clear what every other person in Lincoln Elementary already knew . . . you didn't give Denise Wolff a rough time without paying for it, with either a bloody nose or a black eye . . . or both.

Now it's true, since her return from Fayrah, Denise had made great progress in controlling her temper. But self-control doesn't come overnight—a fact that the blond-haired kid would become painfully aware of.

"In the future, Denny," Mrs. Barnick said, "I suggest you do your sleeping at home."

"Yes, ma'am," Denise mumbled just as the bell to end class rang.

She gathered her books and crowded toward the door with the rest of the kids, where she received the usual "way to go's" and "nice work" from the ones who liked risking their lives. But it really wasn't her fault. She wasn't the one who'd put English at the end of the day. Who in their right mind would schedule the world's most boring subject for sixth period? No, make that the second most boring subject. She'd almost forgotten about math.

Another Day, Another Full Moon

"But she scores so high on the tests," the counselor had told her mother. "If she'd just apply herself she'd be an *A* student," her teachers had said.

"Yeah? Well, let them try being me for a day," Denise muttered as she shuffled down the hall toward her locker. "That would show 'em."

Instinctively she glanced around the hall for the blond-haired kid. But he was no fool. Already he was heading for the exit. Already he knew it was best to stay out of her way—at least for the next couple decades.

Denise arrived at her locker and threw open the door. She began loading up with the evening's torture of homework when the thought suddenly struck her. *Wait a minute! Tonight's the night! Tonight we use the Bloodstone to signal Aristophenix. Tonight I'll finally prove to Joshua that it wasn't just make-believe, or mass hysteria or, how did he put it? . . . "A couple kids' overactive imaginations."*

With dramatic flair, she dumped the books back into her locker, slammed it shut, and headed for the next building—the middle school's gymnasium. That's where the older kids would be setting up their science projects. And since it involved science, that, of course, is where Josh O'Brien would be.

"Hey, Denny!" It was Nathan, Josh's little brother. She slowed down to let him catch up. His limp was just as painful to watch as ever. They'd both hoped it would disappear after their trip to Fayrah, after Denise had seen him without it in the stream's reflection. No such luck. It was still there, just as obvious as ever. But there were other changes. As with Denise, there were deeper changes. . . .

For starters, Nathan was no longer the most selfish human on the face of the planet. Oh, he still had his moments. Like Denise,

3

there were still plenty of areas that needed work. But instead of some modern-day Scrooge, he was coming off more like your average, run-of-the-mill corporate CEO. Not a great improvement, but a start.

"Listen," he said, "I might be late tonight."

"What?" Denise came to a stop. "Tonight's the full moon. If we don't signal them tonight—" She spotted a group of kids straining to eavesdrop and lowered her voice. "If we don't signal them tonight we'll have to wait a whole 'nother month before—"

"I know, I know." Nathan interrupted. "But we're having a geography test tomorrow."

"So?"

"So Jerry Boleslavski's having a lousy time memorizing his state capitals."

"So?"

"So I'd promised to help."

"Nathan . . ."

"How'd I know our teacher was going to spring the test on us tomorrow?"

Denise took a deep breath. She was not going to get angry. Worse things than this had happened, she was sure of it . . . although at the moment she couldn't exactly put her finger on one.

"Look," Nathan said. "We'll get done in time, no sweat. But if I'm not there, you and Josh go ahead without me."

"Nathan . . ."

"I'm serious. There'll be other full moons."

"Nathan . . ."

Without a word, he turned his back on her and hobbled down the hall.

"Nathan . . . Nathaniel!"

Another Day, Another Full Moon

There was no answer.

Denise let out a sigh. Why'd he have to choose tonight to get all compassionate and help a friend?

◻

"I just don't want you to be too disappointed when nothing happens," Joshua said.

"Oh, I won't be," Denise answered as they rounded the corner and headed up the street toward Grandpa O'Brien's Secondhand Shop. She couldn't help grinning as she fingered the Bloodstone inside her coat pocket. The full moon was already high over their heads. In just a few minutes, she'd be exposing the stone to its light. Then she'd see what ol' Josh had to say about "disappointments."

For the past couple hours, he'd had been dragging her all around to see the different science projects, explaining what they were about and how they worked. Joshua loved science, and for him the hours flew. Denise hated science, and for her the hours crawled. But it wasn't a complete waste—during that time she had mastered the fine art of faking interest. In fact, she'd become quite an expert at using phrases like, "No kidding," "I see," "That's neat," and the ever-popular, "Uh-huh."

Denise didn't mind. Faking interest was a small price to pay for Josh's friendship—a friendship that lasted almost as long as she could remember. It lasted through those awful months after her dad left home . . . it lasted through her slowly but surely becoming one of the school's oddballs . . . it even lasted through Josh having to drag her off of wise-cracking bullies whose faces she kept pulverizing.

Yes, sir, if anybody qualified as a friend, it was Joshua O'Brien. The only problem was, he qualified as everybody's friend. He made sure of it. Smart, athletic, funny—he worked very hard at being popular. And if there was anything that drove Denise crazy, it was probably that. Still, his focus on being popular was a minor annoyance that she'd learned to live with.

"Look, I'm not saying something didn't happen to you and Nathan," he continued, "something emotional or even some sort of natural phenomena. But all this talk about a kingdom and Imager and stuff—well, no offense, but it's just a little too far out there for me."

"And you don't believe in anything too far out."

"I believe in science—in cause and effect. But if you're expecting me to buy some sort of magic performed by some sort of"—he searched for the word—"wizard in the sky, sorry, but I'm going to have to pass."

Denise smiled weakly. To be honest she didn't know much about this "wizard in the sky" guy either. Oh sure, everyone in Fayrah had talked about Imager—how he loved them and took a special interest in their lives. But she'd never seen him. In fact, she hadn't even been allowed to enter his city. Even if he did exist, she suspected he'd never have anything to do with her—not Denise Wolff—not the Lincoln Elementary all-school oddball.

The two of them finally arrived at the Secondhand Shop. Joshua pushed open the door, and the bell above gave a little jingle as they stepped inside.

"Hey, Gramps," Joshua called, "we're here."

A stout old man with thin, graying hair shuffled out from behind the row of secondhand toasters. "Good evenin' to you, Joshua," he said. "Oh, and you brought Denny with you, too—what a fine thing."

"Hi, Grandpa." Denise grinned. She always wound up grinning when she talked to the old man. Then, glancing around the shop, she asked, "Did Nathan show up yet?"

Another Day, Another Full Moon

"I haven't seen hide nor hair of him."

"Great," Denise sighed. If he didn't show up soon, she and Joshua would have to go without him. Now that they were safe inside the shop, away from the moonlight, she pulled out the Bloodstone. She fiddled with it nervously, dropping it back and forth in her hands.

Unfortunately the bad news had just begun . . .

"Listen, lad," Grandpa said to Josh. "I won't be needin' you to close the store tonight after all."

"No?"

The old man shook his head. "They've released Mrs. Thomas from the hospital this afternoon, so I won't be goin' to visit her."

Denise spun to Joshua in concern. But he didn't notice. He just shrugged and said, "No problem."

But it was a problem. A *big* problem! How could she signal for the Fayrahnians to come with Grandpa right there in the store? The creatures had barely missed giving the old guy a heart attack the last time they popped in. What would stop it from happening this time around?

Terrific, Denise thought. *First, no Nathan, and now no Fayrahnians. What else could go wrong?*

Unfortunately, she was about to find out . . .

Even though she was inside the shop, and was careful to stay away from the windows, Denise had made one little mistake. When she had pulled the Bloodstone from her pocket and nervously fiddled with it, she hadn't noticed the reflection on the pots and pans in the display window. She hadn't noticed the glint of moonlight that hit the bottom of one of the pots and reflected in her direction. She hadn't noticed that single glint of moonlight that struck the Bloodstone.

That is, until the rock in her hands started to glow . . .

Chapter Two

Just Like Old Times . . . Sorta

First Denise tried to stuff the rock back into her coat pocket. But her coat pocket started to glow.

Next she sidled up to one of the drawers behind the counter. When no one was looking, she yanked it open, dumped the rock inside, and slammed it shut. A good idea, until the drawer started to glow.

Things were not looking good. She leaned against the drawer to cover the glow with her body while at the same time trying to get Joshua's attention. If she could just get him to take Grandpa out of the room for a minute. Forget a minute, she'd settle for five seconds. But, no. He was too busy with some stupid conversation about sports or school or something. *Figures*, she thought. *Let him stand around having a good time while I'm over here trying to save his grandfather from the world's biggest heart attack.*

She began to whistle. Not a bad plan—get Josh's attention and appear to be casual all at the same time. The only problem was Denise knew nothing about whistling. Never had. So instead of a casual little tune, the only sound that came from her mouth was wet, puckering wheezes.

Next, she tried drumming her fingers on the counter. Maybe that would get his attention.

Maybe not.

By now the entire top of the counter had started to glow. So she did what any intelligent person would do. She hopped up on the counter and tried to hide the light with her body. First she sat this way, then that. But the light just kept on spreading until she had to lie down and completely stretch out across the counter top.

So there she was—sprawled out on the counter, noisily drumming her fingers, while puckering and wheezing a pathetic whistle. And then it happened. It was fainter than normal but there was no mistaking the clear . . .

BEEP!........BOP!........BLEEP!.......BURP!....

. . . of Listro Q's Cross-Dimensionalizer.

She'd been expecting it. What she didn't expect was the crashing and banging that followed—the crashing and banging that came from the alley out back.

"What on earth?!" Grandpa exclaimed.

"Prowlers?" Joshua asked.

"We'll see about that," Grandpa said as he reached under the counter for his nightstick. It was only then that he spotted Denise. By now the glow had completely vanished, but she still lay on the counter. "And would you mind tellin' me what you're up to?" he asked her.

"Oh." She quickly sat up. "I was just, uh . . . tired. Yeah, I was tired and thought I'd, uh"—she faked a little yawn—"you know, get some rest."

Grandpa and Josh looked at each other. It was clear neither of them had bought the lie, but before they could question her further, there was more outside banging followed by strange voices—strange, arguing voices.

With nightstick in hand, Grandpa turned and headed for the back door. "Who's out there?" he shouted. "Who's out there, I say? What's going on?"

"Stop him!" Denise whispered to Josh.

"What?"

"Those are the Fayrahnians—I'm sure of it."

Joshua stared at her.

She heard Grandpa throw open the back door. "What are you— " Suddenly his yell froze in midsentence.

"We've got to stop him," Denise cried as she hopped off the counter and started for the back.

But Joshua didn't follow.

"Josh?"

The boy didn't budge. In fact he wasn't moving at all. He just kept staring straight ahead.

"Joshua?"

Still no response.

She crossed to him. "Joshua, what's wrong? Josh, can you hear me?"

But he didn't move. Not a muscle. Not an eyelid. It was as if he had suddenly been frozen. She took a step or two closer and waved her hand in front of his face.

Nothing.

> **It ain't our wish,**
> **the wrong way to be rubbin'.**
> **But we ain't used to welcomes,**
> **with yellin's and clubbin's.**

Denise immediately recognized the awful poetry. "Aristophenix!" she shouted as she spun around to see the furry, bearlike creature enter, complete with his walking stick, checkered vest, and straw hat. Behind him loped Listro Q, just as tall and purple and cool as always. Without another word she raced to them and gave them both a hug . . . but only for a second.

"Whew," she said, quickly pulling away. "What's that smell?"

Aristophenix rolled his eyes over to Listro Q.

The cool purple dude glanced at the floor, cleared his throat, and finally replied. His speech was as scrambled and backward as ever. "Trouble still a little, with Cross-Dimensionalizer, have I."

"So?" Denise asked.

Aristophenix answered,

> **So the wrong coordinates,**
> **he entered again.**
> **So instead of this room,**
> **the garbage bin we landed in.**

Denise burst out laughing. She wasn't sure which was worse—Listro Q's sense of direction or Aristophenix's awful rhymes. Maybe it was a tie. "But, Samson," she asked, looking around for her favorite of the group—the cute bug with the glowing red tail. "Where's Samson?"

> **The little guy got married**
> **to a sweet thing who's dear.**
> **And in Fayrah after weddings,**
> **you don't work for a year.**

"That's great!" Denise exclaimed. "So Sammy got married? That's terrific." She tried her best to sound excited, but she didn't quite pull it off. She'd really gotten to love the little guy during their last journey together. The fact that their personalities were so similar had a lot to do with it. Now they were saying he was married? Well, that was great. A part of Denise was really happy for him. But there was another part of her—a part that felt just a little bit sad, just a little left out.

Speaking of "left out," she suddenly remembered Joshua and spun back to him. "Is he going to be all right?" she asked. "I mean just standing there frozen like that?"

> **He and his grandpa**
> **are doin' just fine.**
> **We've accelerated our clocks**
> **past the speed of their time.**

"What?" Denise didn't quite catch the drift.

"Grab there pot," Listro Q said, pointing to the teapot that sat on the shelf behind her.

She looked at him a moment, then reached for it.

"Drop now it."

Denise hesitated, not entirely understanding. He nodded for her to go ahead. With a shrug, she let the teapot drop. But it didn't drop. It just hung in midair.

"How're you doing that?" she asked in amazement. "How're you making it float?"

Aristophenix answered,

> **It ain't floatin' at all,**
> **quite factually, it's fallin'.**
> **We're just speedin' so fast,**
> **that by our time it's crawlin'.**

"No kidding," Denise said as she grabbed the teapot and let it go again. The results were the same. It just hung there.

"So Grandpa and Josh aren't frozen? We're just moving faster than they are?"

"Correct are you," Listro Q answered.

Just Like Old Times . . . Sorta

"But I wanted Josh to come with us," Denise said. "He doesn't believe in any of this stuff and I wanted him to come see for—"

Aristophenix politely interrupted,

> **We understand the problem;**
> **we've been to the Weaver.**
> **When it comes to Imager,**
> **Josh ain't no believer.**

Denise nodded. That was it in a nutshell. She wasn't sure what they meant about the "Weaver," but they were right about Josh refusing to believe in Imager.

"Worry not to," Listro Q assured her. "Coming with us will be he." Then, with a smile, he added, "But that's all not."

Denise waited for more.

"A problem says the Weaver still have you."

"Me?" Denise asked.

"How loved by Imager are you. Still understand not do you."

Denise opened her mouth to argue but stopped. It wouldn't do any good. Whoever this Weaver guy was, he had her figured out just as well as he had Joshua. It was true. When it came to Imager, Denise knew there had to be somebody out there running the show. After all that she'd seen and heard on her last trip, she knew that much. But for Imager, to actually *like* her, to take a personal interest in her, when he was so awesome and powerful—well, to her it sounded like a lot of wishful thinking—a nice idea, but definitely fantasy time.

Yet, according to Listro Q, this sounded like another reason they had come—to prove to her it *wasn't* fantasy.

**So pack up yer bags,
let's get ready to shove.
For Josh it's the proof,
for you it's the love.**

"What about Nathan?" Denise suddenly remembered. "He wanted to come, too."

"Later come can he. But now move must we."

Denise hesitated, then gave Listro Q a nod. After their last adventure together, she knew he could be trusted.

Without further ado, he reached for the little remote control box, pressed four buttons . . .

BEEP!........BOP!........BLEEP!.......BURP!....

. . . and they were off.

Suddenly the room filled with blinding light. And then, just as suddenly, there was no room at all—just the light. As with the last trip, Denise felt herself falling. Once again she looked around and saw thousands of bright, multicolored lights—all falling toward a city of much brighter lights below—all falling toward the Center, Imager's home.

It took a moment for her eyes to adjust to the brightness. But soon she could make out the glowing forms of Aristophenix and Listro Q beside her. They were quietly speaking to Joshua—at least she thought it was Joshua. But this Joshua was bigger and more powerful—especially in his shoulders. He had to be, because in each of his thick, muscular arms he carried a huge clay pot, filled to the brim with water—but not the water of earth. It was the water from Fayrah's stream—the water made up of the liquid letters and words.

Just Like Old Times . . . Sorta

So, you're finally with us, Josh spoke as he grinned at Denise. But he really wasn't speaking—it was more like he was thinking.

What do you mean? she thought back.

Speeded up his time past yours did we, Listro Q explained. *To tell him everything, so frightened not be he.*

Denise nodded though she wasn't thrilled about the idea. It was one thing to zip around somebody else who was frozen. But to be the frozen one was different. Who knew what type of idiot expression she'd had stuck on her face or for how long it had been stuck there?

Don't worry, Josh thought back as if he'd read her mind. *You looked incredible . . . you still do!*

Denise shot him an angry look. It wasn't like Josh to be mean. But when she saw his eyes, she realized he wasn't teasing. Instead, he looked at her with a type of . . . well, the only word she could think of to describe it was . . . *admiration.*

Flustered and caught off guard, Denise glanced down and immediately saw the reason for Joshua's comment. Once again, she was wearing the gorgeous wedding gown—the gown she had seen in the stream—the one made of the intricate lace and tiny glowing pearls. But the pearls weren't all that glowed. She could feel color racing to her cheeks. It was an amazing fact, but she had actually been complimented for her looks. And, worse yet, she was actually blushing over it!

Not sure what to say or what to do, she avoided the topic altogether. Turning to the Fayrahnians she asked, *Did you guys tell him about the Center? Did you tell him what he has to do to cross through?*

But neither Listro Q nor Aristophenix answered. Their eyes were already closed and their heads were tilted back. Already they were beginning to quietly speak words of love and appreciation for Imager.

Yeah, they told me, Joshua volunteered. *I'm supposed to think of happy stuff—maybe sing a song.*

No, more than that! Denise thought. Suddenly memories of the last time she tried to enter the Center rushed in. Awful, terrifying memories. Memories of being flung into an empty darkness. *You've got to sing one of your grandpa's songs. That's what Nathan did. The only way he made it through was by singing one of your grandpa's old Irish hymns.*

A look of concern crossed Josh's face. *A hymn?*

Denise nodded and looked down. The Center was quickly approaching. Already she could make out the bright glowing buildings. Already she could see the thin layer of fog that formed the subtle but impenetrable barrier.

I don't know, Denny—I don't remember any hymn.

Denise felt a wave of panic. And with the panic came the first vibrations. They were faint, but rapidly increasing.

Sure you do, she insisted, trying to push back the fear. *He used to sing it to you guys at bedtime.*

A hymn? I don't think . . .

The vibrating grew worse, turning into a shaking which became more and more violent.

Come on, Joshua! she urged. There was no mistaking the fear she felt. *You've got to remember!*

The scowl deepened on Josh's face.

Denise cast another look below. They were practically at the Center. Already the shaking was turning into teeth-rattling knocks and bone-jarring bounces. Any moment they would enter the fog where the shaking would increase a thousand times, where it would turn into violent lurching and lunging. But that would only last a second. Then they would be yanked to a screeching stop—

and, without warning, hurtled in the opposite direction, back past the Secondhand Store and out into a black void—an empty blackness that was full of nothing but fear and even darker blackness.

Come on Joshua! Denise's mind cried. *Think!* She would not experience the terror of that darkness again—she *could* not. *THINK! THINK!*

The bouncings and bangings became nightmarish—like a carnival ride out of control, growing worse by the second!

Then she heard it. It was slow and halting at first, but it quickly grew in volume and confidence . . .

"Be thou . . . my vision, O Lord . . . of my . . . heart."

Josh was starting to sing! Sometimes there were pauses or he would hum if he couldn't remember the words. But he pressed on. . . .

"Naught be all else . . . mm-mm-mmmmm that thou art."

That's it, Josh! Denise cried. *Keep it up! Keep it up!*

"Thou my best thought . . . by day or by night. Mmm-mm mmm mmmm-mm, thy presence my light."

The shaking grew less . . . and just in time! Immediately they dropped into the first wispy layers of the Center. Denise closed her eyes and forced herself to concentrate on the words. Eventually she tried to join in—half singing, half humming . . . as Josh continued . . .

"Be thou my wisdom, mmm-mm my true word, Mm mm-mm mmm mmmmm and thou with me, Lord."

The shaking continued to decrease.

"Thou my great Father and I thy true Son. Thou in me dwelleth and I with thee one."

Finally the shaking stopped altogether. They had passed through—Denise knew it. Even with eyes closed, she could tell everything was much brighter now—*much* brighter. She was tempted to open her eyes but she didn't. She knew the sight would fill her with fear—and with that fear the awful shaking would return.

At last she felt the pressure of something under her feet. They had landed! They had landed at the Center! Still, she was afraid to open her eyes—afraid of what she might see. Yet she knew she'd hate herself forever if she didn't take one look . . . at least one little peek.

Chapter Three

Arrivals

As Denise and the guys landed at the Center, a welcoming party was preparing for their arrival just five dimensions away. The vice-governor of Biiq sat at his banquet table, giving last-minute instructions to Bud, one of the greatest scientists in the realm. "Click   clickCLICK   CLICKclick   CLICKCLICKclick   click CLICKclick."

Nearly 150 epochs had passed since they quit using words in Biiq. Words were so inaccurate when it came to real communication. And in Biiq, a kingdom of math and science, accuracy was supreme. So, instead of words, everyone simply clicked their tongues. The pauses between clicks, the number of clicks, and the loudness of each click said it all. Of course it made their poetry a little difficult to appreciate . . . but they were scientists. What did they care about verse or rhyme?

Information had arrived earlier from the Weaver. Biiq would finally play host to the two precious threads from the Upside-Down Kingdom. One thread, a female, knew of Imager but did not understand his love. The other, a male, refused to believe in Imager at all because it supposedly went against the laws of logic and science.

That argument always made Bud chuckle. It was *because* of Imager's infinite logic and awesome science that the Kingdom of Biiq was created in the first place. Here, people could spend their entire life exploring Imager—understanding him through mathematical formulas, marveling over him through scientific investigation. Here, people could understand and experience Imager more deeply than anyplace in the universe! Of course, the boys over in the art kingdoms might not entirely agree, but who cared. Today they were the ones to help the Upside Downers. *Their* kingdom was the one privileged to draw them closer to Imager's heart.

For several epochs Bud had been in charge of building the special laboratory called the Machine. Throughout that time, rumors had spread far and wide regarding who the Machine was being built for and when it would be used. Well, today those rumors would finally be put to rest.

The Machine was designed for the two Upside Downers, particularly for the one who didn't understand Imager's love. And now the vice-governor was giving Bud last-minute instructions on welcoming the Upside Downers to his kingdom and introducing them to the wonderful new invention.

Bud received his orders with an enthusiastic, "CLICKclick click CLICK clickCLICK," then turned and immediately fell over the nearest chair. Now that wouldn't have been a problem. Folks around the palace were used to Bud being a little—how did they say it?—*heavy on his feet*? But when he jumped up and crashed into the waiter carrying the vice-governor's mashed potatoes and mustard gravy . . . then spun around, tripped, and landed face first into the vice-governor's cream of caramel soup, well, it was bordering on being a problem.

The vice-governor stared down at Bud and pursed his lips in self-control.

Bud stared up from the soup and tried to smile. Then, without a word, he rose, wrung out his mustache, gave a weak sort of salute, and raced out of the palace for all he was worth. It's not that he was embarrassed. Such catastrophes were normal for Bud—too normal. He may have been one of Biiq's greatest scientists, but he was also one of Biiq's greatest clods. He was in a hurry

Arrivals

because the Upside Downers were about to arrive. They'd only make a brief stop at the Center. Since neither of them were re-Breathed, they couldn't stay there long—Imager's presence would destroy them. So Bud raced off to make final preparations. There was much to do and little time to do it.

◙

Denise's first impression of the Center was the blinding white light. Her second was the singing. It was not your average, run-of-the-mill choir stuff. It was a swelling, breathtaking, send-shivers-up-your-spine type of singing. In fact, it was so beautiful and awe-inspiring that before she knew it, a lump had formed in her throat.

At first Denise thought the song came from the various light-creatures that were strolling past her. But once she grew accustomed to the city's brilliance, she saw that the light-creatures weren't the only ones doing the singing. It came from every-where—the buildings, the streets, the trees, even the blades of grass (a neat trick since none of these things had mouths). Still, somehow, some way, everything seemed to be singing.

But that was just one way the song was different. Another was that Denise not only heard it, but she *felt* it . . . inside her. Somehow the notes did more than enter her ears. They seeped into her whole body, resonating in her muscles, her organs, her bones. It was as if all of her insides had joined in the song.

Aristophenix grinned at the puzzled look on her face and explained,

All that's of Imager,
vibrates with his voice.
From stars to dirt clods,
all sing and rejoice.

Denise nodded, pretending to understand. Then something even stranger happened. Tears began filling her eyes . . . and for once in her life, she didn't try to stop them. Suddenly, all she wanted was to sit down on the glowing street and have a good cry. But not a cry of sadness . . . these were tears of joy. Imagine Denise Wolff wanting to sit down on the ground and cry for joy. Amazing!

She couldn't put her finger on it, but she suspected that the emotion had something to do with the song. Because as she felt herself joining in, she also felt something else. For the very first time in her life, Denise began to feel like she "belonged." It was a wonderful feeling. After all these years of searching to fit in and be accepted, Denise finally felt that she was . . . well, the word that kept coming to her mind was . . . *home*. Denise finally felt that she was *home*.

She glanced over at Josh beside her. He was crying, too. Good. That meant she wasn't totally out of her mind. Or was she? Because now she noticed something even stranger. She could see through him! Not clearly, mind you. It was more like looking at a stained-glass window. Josh's form and color were still there, along with most of the details. But now she could actually see some of the light-creatures moving behind him!

She raised her arm to look at her own hand. It was the same thing! *Oh, brother*, she thought, *now what's going on?* She looked to Aristophenix for an answer, but it was Listro Q's turn to explain.

"Super reality is the Center. Everything else is shadow of it."

Again she looked at her hand. He was right. Because she wasn't glowing like the rest of the Center and because she seemed to be transparent, she looked like . . . well, she really did look like a shadow.

The thought didn't exactly thrill her. But it didn't upset her either. Not here. Not with all of this joy and goodness and wonder.

Arrivals

She glanced at the passing light-creatures. Whenever she looked straight at them, all she saw was a blazing glare of light. But when she looked away and caught them out of the corner of her eye, she could make out some of their details—details that showed these little creatures really weren't creatures at all.

Like the light that was approaching her now. How could it be living? When she glanced off to the side all she saw was a hammock—that's right, a swinging hammock. But not just any swinging hammock. No, sir. It was the very same hammock that hung in her uncle's apple orchard! She was certain of it. It was the very same hammock that she, her mom, and her dad used to romp and play in—the same one that held all those wonderful memories of their times together, back when they *were* together.

As it passed by her, Denise tried to see who was in it, but with little success. Every time she looked directly at the hammock, the whole thing blurred back into a glare of brightness.

Then there were the sounds . . . laughing, giggling, and shouting. She recognized the voices immediately. They were her parents' . . . and herself. In fact, for a moment Denise actually felt like she was back in that hammock, nestled between her parents' loving arms. The joy was impossible to describe. She looked at Aristophenix.

He smiled and answered,

**Reality of the Center,
your logical mind cannot grasp.
So your brain sees in symbols,
to help lighten the task.**

It was tough to find her voice with all of the emotion racing through her, but at last Denise was able to speak. "You mean that's not my uncle's hammock?"

"A hammock?" Aristophenix chuckled lightly. "Ask Joshua."

"No way," Josh whispered in awe as he watched the same light-creature pass. "That's my whole Little League baseball team back in fifth grade—back when we won the All-City Championship."

"Right," she laughed. "Your whole Little League baseball team." But when she looked at him she saw he wasn't joking. In fact, his face glowed with as much joy as hers. He obviously saw the light-creature as one thing while she saw it as something entirely different. But, whatever they saw, it made them feel exactly the same . . . wonderful, warm, and incredibly happy.

She turned back toward the hammock or Little League team or whatever it was. Now it was farther down the road and beginning to look like all the other glowing lights. Any detail she had seen was swallowed up by the overall glare. But it wasn't just the glare of the light-creature. It was also the glare from the horizon. Because just over the ridge was a light so radiant, so brilliant, that it made all of the other lights dim by comparison.

But it was more than just light. There was something different about this light. It had a type of *splendor* about it. A type of . . . *glory*. A glory so intense that it made Denise catch her breath.

Her heart began pounding in her chest. She breathed faster. No one had to tell her. Now she knew what the singing was about. Just over that ridge was the source of all the Center's light, all the Center's beauty, and all the Center's glory. Just over that ridge she knew she would finally see . . . Imager.

Without a word she started up the path toward the top of the knoll.

Aristophenix spotted her and cried out, "Denny, no!"

But Denise barely heard. She picked up her pace—breaking into a run.

24

Arrivals

Listro Q took off after her. "No! Denny! Back come here!"

But she wasn't listening. All she could do was stare at the light blazing from behind the ridge. It burned her eyes, making the back of them ache, but she would not stop looking . . . or running.

Listro Q caught up to her and ran beside her. "Denny!" he shouted. "Stop must you!"

"Why?" she puffed, refusing to take her eyes off the approaching ridge.

"As close to this, dare get you!"

"Why?" she repeated, still not looking at him, still running for all she was worth.

"Re-Breathed not are you! Destroy you will his presence!"

If Denise had any extra air in her lungs she would have broken out laughing. "No way!" she panted. "I feel his love now. I finally see what you and Aristophenix have been saying!"

"But . . ." Listro Q was sounding desperate. "Unapproachable is he! Too pure for you is he!"

They passed other light-creatures that were heading toward the ridge—first the hammock, and then one creature after another as Denise continued to press on. Her lungs started to burn, crying out for more air. But she was nearly there. Nearly at the top of the hill.

The music grew louder. Denise's joy increased until she could barely think. The song was everywhere—inside her, overpowering her, consuming her.

And the light. It was so bright that it was all she could see. It was all she wanted to see. If Listro Q was still shouting, she wasn't listening. If her feet were still touching the path, she wasn't feeling it. There was only light. Then her thoughts began to dissolve. One concept after another slipped away. She tried remembering her name and couldn't. Her thoughts, her memories, her very identity were . . . vanishing. But it didn't matter, because there was only the light.

Stumbling, she glanced down and saw that her body was also disappearing! Vanishing memories! Vanishing thoughts! Vanishing body! Everything about Denise was vanishing! With every step she took toward the light, less and less of her existed!

"Denny! Listen to me you!" Listro Q cried. But she barely heard, nor did she care. There was only the light.

Then it happened. The unthinkable. Denise ran straight through one of the light-creatures. She had grown so unreal that she was able to pass through solid objects! It was as if she had become vapor. And with every step she took, more and more of her faded.

In desperation, Listro Q leapt at her. He grabbed her waist and tried tackling her to the ground.

But he fell to the path alone. Her body had passed completely through his arms.

"*Denny*!" he cried.

But Denise no longer heard. She no longer cared.

She no longer existed.

Chapter Four

The Weaver

"Nine hours," Josh complained as he paced the gleaming white marble floor. "How much longer?" He threw another glance toward glass and steel doors. They had remained tightly shut ever since their arrival—ever since an emergency team had raced through them with the last remaining vapors they had recovered of Denise.

For the past several hours Josh had been eyeing those doors, studying the stark black letters that read:

**RESTRICTED AREA
ENTRANCE PROHIBITED**

And, with the passing of each hour, Joshua grew more certain that, *restricted* or not, he was going to have to break through those doors to find his friend. It was just a matter of time . . . and of getting past the two huge elklike guards who blocked the double doors with their antlers.

Aristophenix stood at the far end of the room near one of the crystal windows. They were in Fayrah now. Listro Q had cross-dimensionalized them over as quickly as possible. And, since Josh was an Upside Downer, Aristophenix had already given him the water from the stream so he could see and hear right side up.

Now the pudgy, bearlike creature gazed out onto the lush courtyard where a hundred Fayrahnians quietly waited . . . and prayed. Denise had been their friend. In fact, many of them had been rescued as a result of her last visit.

THE **IMAGER CHRONICLES**

Aristophenix raised his eyes from the crowd to look at the distant Blood Mountains. They glowed and pulsed the way they always did when citizens of the Upside-Down Kingdom were present. "I shouldn't of taken ya there," he sighed heavily. "Until you were both re-Breathed, I should never have taken ya there."

Suddenly the doors leading to the courtyard flew open. Two Fayrahnians raced in. One looked exactly like Aristophenix—except for the four ears and two noses. The other looked like a walking seahorse with legs. Between them they carried a long hollow tube with something glowing inside it.

"More threads from the Center!" the seahorse cried. Immediately the Elk Guards stepped aside as the sealed doors whisked open.

It was now or never.

In a flash, Josh made his move.

"Joshua!" Aristophenix called.

But it was too late. Josh broke past the guards and ran down the glaring white hallway for all he was worth.

"Stop him!" the seahorse shouted. "He must not see her tapestry!"

The two guards galloped down the hallway after him, the sound of their hooves echoing against the marble walls and floor.

Josh glanced over his shoulder. They were gaining on him. No way was he a match for their powerful legs.

But he continued to run. He wasn't worried about being hurt. He knew that wasn't the Fayrahnian way. He *was* worried about the Elks leaping over him and blocking his path with their giant antlers.

The opening to a huge room lay just ahead. Josh bore down, straining with every muscle. Suddenly the clatter of hooves stopped. He looked up to see that they had jumped and were sailing high over his head. In a moment they'd land in front of him

The Weaver

and block his rescue. He had no choice. He did what any ex-All City Little League Champion would do. He threw out his feet, leaned back, and slid across the marble floor!

It worked perfectly. The Elks landed in front of him but had no time to drop their antlers and block him. He slid right between their legs and into the room.

He leaped to his feet but quickly came to a stop. He was in some sort of giant lecture hall. He stood on a balcony overlooking hundreds of different creatures. Hundreds of different Fayrahnians who, because of his disturbance, were all looking right back at him.

Well, all but one.

In the center of the hall was a single man wearing what looked like a blacksmith's apron. He was old and balding. What hair he did have was gray and flyaway. He was hunched over and concentrating on an old-fashioned loom used for weaving. But the threads were no ordinary threads. They glowed. And not with ordinary light. These threads glowed with the same brilliance and beauty as the light from the Center. And the pattern the old man was weaving? It shimmered and sparkled with such depth and beauty that it made Joshua's chest ache.

"Bring him here," the Weaver ordered. He never looked up but kept concentrating on the pattern before him.

"But, Weaver," the seahorse called. "He knows the girl, he must not see."

"It is too late, yes, it is," the Weaver answered. "Bring him here."

The Elk guards exchanged anxious looks. Apparently approaching the Weaver as he worked was not something they relished. Luckily for them Aristophenix waddled into the room, huffing and puffing a storm.

> **The error was (pant, pant) all mine,**
> **to this (pant) I confess.**
> **I'll take him (pant, pant) down to the Weaver**
> **and (pant) clear up all this mess.**

The guards didn't have to be asked twice. Gratefully, they stepped back.

Still gasping for breath, Aristophenix came forward and took hold of Josh's arm. Well, to most it looked like he took hold of it. Actually, it was Josh who was doing the holding as he supported the exhausted bear. Together they started down the stairs toward the Weaver.

A moment later Listro Q stepped in to join them. Aristophenix turned to him and spoke in a hushed whisper.

> **What are ya doin'?**
> **Don't be a sap.**
> **As the leader it's me,**
> **who should be takin' the rap.**

Listro Q only smiled. "Cool," was all he said.

Joshua looked on, impressed. Listro Q *was* cool. Cool and loyal. But right now Josh was more concerned about Denise. She was down there somewhere. And he had to help her. But where could she have—

And then he spotted it. Far from the Weaver, at the other end of the room. On a table beneath intense, glaring lights. It was the faintest outline of a human body.

"Denny!" Josh gasped.

"Correct," Listro Q whispered as they continued down the steps.

"But . . . why isn't anybody with her?" Josh demanded.

The Weaver

"They're all with the Weaver when they should be at that other table trying to save Denny!"

Listro Q tried to explain. "Physical body of hers only at that table is it." He pointed to the table where Denise's remains lay. "But her *character*," he said, pointing to the Weaver and his loom, "her character over there is."

"What are you talking about?" Josh argued. He motioned toward the glowing pattern on the Weaver's loom. "That's just some stupid design he's making."

Aristophenix patiently explained,

> **That design is her life.**
> **Each Fiber and strand**
> **is woven together,**
> **as Imager planned.**

Josh stared at him. He knew his mouth was hanging open but he didn't much care. "You mean, *that* . . ." He pointed at the design on the loom. "*That's* her life—that pattern is who she is?"

Aristophenix nodded.

> **Each thread is a moment**
> **in her life's master plan,**
> **to create a character,**
> **both glorious and grand.**

Josh continued to stare at the pattern that was forming. Aristophenix was right. It *was* "glorious." It *was* "grand." No wonder he was so moved when he first saw it. But there was something else . . .

The more Josh stared at the pattern, the more it began to make sense. Somehow the design really was Denise. Not her body, not what she looked like on the outside—but how she was on the inside . . . her character, her personality. Somehow the pattern that was appearing on the loom was what Denise was like as a person.

Then Josh saw something else. "Wait a minute!" he cried. "What's that?"

The Weaver had picked up a dark ugly thread and was adding it to the pattern. It was an awful, sinister color, so repulsive that it made Josh shudder. Such ugly darkness had no place with such beauty. In fact it looked like the Weaver was about to destroy his wonderful work by adding the awful-looking thread.

"What are you doing?" Josh shouted. By now they had reached the bottom of the steps. They were only a few yards from the loom. "Stop it, you're ruining it!"

Everyone tensed as Josh's voice echoed about the hall—everyone but the Weaver. For a moment the old man did not answer but remained hunched over the loom, carefully working in the dark, ominous thread. When he did speak, it was only one sentence. And he did not look up.

"This thread will give her strength and depth, yes, it will."

But Josh barely heard. He couldn't take his eyes off the thread. It was hideous. If this pattern, this tapestry, really was Denise's life, that thread would bring her incredible pain, unbearable heartache. Even now, as the Weaver continued to work it into the pattern, it seemed to fight against and destroy the beauty of all the other threads, ruining the entire design.

"Stop it! You're hurting her!"

But the Weaver kept right on working.

Joshua had to do something. He couldn't just stand around and let the old man destroy his friend's life. He pulled his arm from Aristophenix and started for the loom. He'd rip that awful thread out of the Weaver's hand if he had to!

But the other Fayrahnians quickly moved to block his path. He tried to push and shove his way through, but there were just too many of them. If he managed to force one aside three more appeared in its place.

Desperately he looked about. There had to be something he could do. *Wait a minute! What about Denny's body? The physical one on the brightly lit table across the room?* There wasn't much of her there—just a faint outline. And of course, it was only the outside of her without her personality. But some of Denise was better than none of her!

Listro Q was the first to see the look in his eyes. "Josh—no!"

But he was too late. Joshua broke across the hall toward the table. The few Fayrahnians that stood between Josh and the table tried to stop him, but he was too fast and too strong. Those he couldn't sidestep, he shoved out of the way as he sprinted toward the table that held the faint, quivering form of Denise's body.

"You don't understand!" Aristophenix shouted. "You'll cripple her character! You'll ruin her!"

For the first time the Weaver glanced up. And for the first time Josh saw a look of concern cross his face. But it lasted only a second. He quickly returned to his task, working faster than ever.

Josh continued forward. Just another twenty feet and a few more Fayrahnians. And then what? He wasn't sure. Maybe he'd scoop up the faint outline of Denise's body and try to escape with it. Anything to get her away from the Weaver and his awful dark thread.

He glanced across the room and saw the Weaver working faster, his nimble fingers moving the dark thread in and out of the strands as quickly as possible. It had become a race. The Weaver desperate to complete his task—Josh desperate to save Denise before he did.

A Fayrahnian reached out and nearly had Josh until he faked a left and expertly spun around to the right.

Now it was a clear shot to Denise.

That is, until the seahorse leaped off the balcony and landed between them. The animal had obviously seen too many movie superheroes and figured this was his big break to become one. Unfortunately, as he landed on the hard floor, the only thing that broke was his ankle. He grabbed it, writhing in agony.

Josh sidestepped the poor fellow and continued his race toward the table.

"Five strands!" someone shouted. "The Weaver has only five strands!"

Josh understood. The Weaver had five strands to go—five strands to finish weaving before the dark thread became a permanent part of Denise's tapestry. He looked up and saw the man's fingers fly.

In and out. In and out.

Josh turned back to Denise. He was practically there. Just two steps to go.

In and out.

He reached the table, raised his arms toward her. She was nearly in his grasp—

"JOSHUA, NO!" Listro Q shouted. "COMPLETE FIRST MUST SHE BE!"

But he paid no attention.

In and out.

And then, just as Josh's hands touched her semitransparent form . . .

In and out.

The Weaver

The crowd broke into cheers. The Weaver had finished! The dark thread was woven into place! The quivering, transparent image of Denise suddenly took shape in Josh's arms—she now had substance—she now had weight.

"Denny!" he cried.

"Joshua," she gasped.

Across the room, the Weaver leaned back in his chair. Removing his spectacles, he grabbed a handkerchief from his coat. It had been close, but he had succeeded. Now he blotted his face with his handkerchief and shook his head.

"Upside Downers," he wearily sighed. "Will they ever learn? . . ."

Chapter Five

A Guided Tour

"Let me get this straight." Josh scowled. "You mean to tell me that you've woven the pattern of every person that's ever lived?"

"That's right, yes, it is . . . and that ever will," the Weaver added.

The scowl deepened as they walked through a series of large, cavernous hallways. On each wall hung hundreds of shimmering tapestries. Each was intricately beautiful, magnificently breathtaking. And each was fashioned from the same glowing threads as Denise's pattern. The whole place was like a giant art museum. But not like the ones that are full of dull, boring masterpieces— the ones they drag you through on school field trips. No way. These were full of life . . . glowing, shimmering, quivering-with-beauty life.

It had been several hours since Denise was revived. Now she walked between Josh and the Weaver as the old man did his best to fill them in on all that had happened.

"How could you keep up?" Denise asked. "I mean, weaving so many people? Where do you find the time?"

"Eternity is a bit longer than you can imagine," the Weaver chuckled. "We had a head start on you."

Josh was still having difficulty. "I'm sorry," he apologized. "This is just a little too weird. I don't think I can buy all of it."

The Weaver gave another gentle chuckle. "I knew that would be a problem, yes, I did. When Imager first asked me to weave that thread into you, I knew you'd have a hard time."

A Guided Tour

"What thread?"

"The logic thread of yours—the one always wanting proof."

Josh and Denise exchanged looks. Whoever this old-timer was, he certainly had Josh figured out.

"But that's okay." The old man smiled as they shuffled out of one hall and into another. "That's part of the plan, yes, it is. That's why your tapestry is in these most honored halls."

"You're kidding?" Josh's voice cracked. He tried again, clearing his throat, attempting to sound more adult. "That is to say, my tapestry, it's here?"

"Of course," the Weaver laughed.

"Well, can I, you know—is it possible to see it?"

"Yeah," Denise joined in.

"Sorry, that's out of the question. Yes, it is."

"Why?"

"An Upside Downer is never pleased with his pattern. No, he isn't. Until his thread, until his design is added to Imager's final tapestry, he always tries to change it."

"I wouldn't do that, I promise." Josh grimaced at the urgency in his voice.

"You wouldn't, you say?"

Again he attempted to sound more adult. "No, of course not. You can trust me."

"Just as I could trust you not to change Denise's tapestry?"

"You saw my tapestry?" Denise asked in astonishment.

Josh ignored her and answered the Weaver. "Well, that was, you know, different."

"You saw my tapestry?" Denise repeated.

"How, different?" the old man asked.

"You were putting in that ugly dark thread."

37

"What thread?" Denise demanded, growing more and more frustrated that no one was answering her.

"The thread will give her character, yes, it will. It will give her—"

"*What thread are you guys talking about?*" Denise's shout echoed inside the giant room. She hadn't meant to be so loud. All she wanted was some attention. Well, she definitely had it. For a moment both of them stared at her as if she'd lost her mind. She smiled weakly and repeated the question a bit more quietly. "Uh, what thread are we, you know, talking about here?"

"There is a reappearing thread in this season of your life, yes, there is," the Weaver explained. "It is dark and it is sinister."

"It's really awful," Josh agreed.

Denise looked first at the Weaver, then at Josh, then back at the Weaver. "Why? I mean, if it's so dark and bad, why do I have to have it?"

It was the Weaver's turn to clear his throat. Apparently he hadn't meant to get into all the details. But Josh had pulled him in, and there was no way to get out but with the truth. "The thread will give you character and depth," he explained. "It will make you one of Imager's most valued creations. Yes, it will."

"But . . . what is it?" Denise asked. "What type of darkness is it?"

The Weaver gave her a careful look. Instead of answering, he slowly came to a stop in front of another glowing and shimmering masterpiece. "Tell me," he asked, "what do you two think of this tapestry?"

"It's terrific," Denise answered. "Just like all the others, but—"

"Take a closer look," he insisted. "Both of you. Step closer and look at the threads."

The two exchanged glances and obeyed.

A Guided Tour

"Are they all the same?" the Weaver asked. "The threads, I mean. Are they all the same colors and brightness?"

"Of course not," Josh answered. "Otherwise the tapestry would be boring; there'd be nothing to it."

The old man smiled at the answer. "I wove you well, Joshua O'Brien." Then, looking back at the tapestry, he continued. "And the darkest thread, do you see it?"

"Yes, it's right there near the center." Denise pointed. "It runs all the way to the bottom."

"Good. Now . . . step back and see how that one thread adds to the overall beauty of the piece."

Once again the two obeyed. And, as they stood staring at the pattern, Denise could see how that one dark thread, woven in and out, created a type of strength, a contrast for the rest of the threads. It seemed to give the entire tapestry its depth, its texture, its great beauty.

"If I would have disobeyed Imager—if I would have refused to add that thread, tell me, what would have happened?"

"The pattern wouldn't work," Denise answered.

Josh agreed. "The tapestry would be nothing without it."

"Right again, yes, you are."

"Who is this person?" Josh asked. "I can't explain it, but the pattern looks—it looks kinda familiar. Do we know him?"

Denise turned to the Weaver. Now that Josh mentioned it, there was something familiar about it.

The Weaver broke into a smile. There was no missing the love he had for his craftsmanship. At last he spoke. "This is your brother . . . Nathan O'Brien."

Denise gasped. It was true. She could see it now. Somehow the pattern of that tapestry perfectly showed Nathan's personality. Not just the spoiled selfish Nathan of a few months ago, but also the new, giving Nathan that had started to emerge. It was amazing—the design really did capture Nathan's character. Completely.

"And that dark thread?" Josh asked.

"The dark thread is Nathan's hip—the deformity that has caused him to limp with such pain over the years."

Denise stared at the tapestry, even more amazed.

The Weaver continued. "Look how all the brighter threads radiate from that darker one. Look how they're highlighted and magnified—how their beauty is intensified. Without that darker thread, the tapestry would have little substance. It would have none of the depth, none of the extraordinary strength that we see."

Denise nodded. It was true. Nathan's greatest handicap, in the hands of the Weaver, had become his greatest strength. Incredible.

The Weaver finished with one last thought. "Imager has great plans for all of you. But sometimes the heart is not big enough to hold such plans—sometimes it must be enlarged through hardship."

The silence lasted several moments. Finally Josh turned back to the Weaver. "But . . . what about Denny's question? You never answered it. What about *her* thread?"

The Weaver looked curiously at Josh. "I'd forgotten your persistence. Perhaps I wove you too well."

Josh continued to wait for his answer.

With a deep sigh the Weaver began, "Denny first met that thread in Keygarp. She saw it circling high above her in the frozen forest."

Denise could feel the hair on her arms begin to rise.

"Since then she has also seen it in her dreams." Turning to her he added, "In fact, the last time you saw it was this afternoon—when you were daydreaming in your sixth period English class."

A Guided Tour

"The witch?" Denise gasped. "That thing flying around with those awful black wings?"

"She's no witch, Denise. She is the *Illusionist*—a queen. That is, until Nathan destroyed her kingdom. In any case, she and the evil Bobok have made a pact. You have been promised to her."

"*Promised* to her?"

The Weaver nodded gravely.

"What are you talking about?!" Denise could feel the tops of her ears growing hot with anger. "Nobody can *promise* me. What do I look like—a baseball card? People can't trade me around without my permission."

"That's right," Josh agreed. "Doesn't she have some say in the matter?"

"Of course she does. Every decision you make is of your own free will. These threads are only the *final* outcome—the ones Imager knows you will eventually choose."

"And he knows I'm going to let myself be given to some ugly, bat-winged queen?"

"No. He knows that your struggle against her will be fierce."

"Will I win?"

The Weaver hesitated. Finally he shook his head. "I cannot answer that, no, I can't. The decision will be yours."

"But you know what I'll decide—you just said so."

"Please . . ." The Weaver motioned toward the doorway at the end of the hall. "They are waiting."

"Who?"

"Your friends, Listro Q and Aristophenix."

"But you haven't answered my quest—"

"I have said too much already."

"But—"

41

He raised his hand for silence. It was a gentle movement but one that made it clear the topic was closed. Starting toward the doorway, he changed the subject altogether. "Your purpose for this journey, has it been fulfilled?"

"What purpose?" Denise asked.

"For Joshua."

"Oh, you mean proving Imager to him?"

The Weaver nodded.

She looked at Josh. Her friend stared hard at the marble floor. She could tell he wanted to be polite, but she could also tell he wanted to be honest.

Finally he spoke, "Everything about this place seems real, I'll give you that. But it's so *different* from the reality we normally experience. How do I know I'm not just having some sort of dream or something?"

Denise let out a sigh of frustration and looked at the Weaver.

But the old man was nodding in quiet understanding. Then he turned to Denise. "And you?" he asked. "You still do not believe Imager's compassion?"

The question caught Denise off guard, until she remembered that was the other reason they'd come. She knew her answer was no better than Josh's so she said nothing, hoping the question would somehow go away.

But the Weaver continued to wait.

Finally she spoke, "How can I believe in his love when"—she swallowed—"when all he does if you try to get close to him is hurt and destroy you?"

The old man nodded, his eyes growing moist. "Then come," he said softly, "we must not be late." With that he turned and resumed shuffling toward the door.

A Guided Tour

Denise and Josh glanced at each other and followed. It appeared that their adventure wasn't quite over . . .

Chapter Six

The Machine

"Clickclick CLICKclickCLICK." Bud continued testing the microphone. He blew into it and stepped a little closer. "click CLICKCLICK." Suddenly the speakers squealed with feedback. The guests surrounding the outdoor stage cringed in pain until the noise stopped and they resumed their smiles and chitchat. After all, that was Bud up there on stage. Such things were expected.

Bud had been told that the Upside Downers had just left Fayrah and were heading for Biiq. They'd had a couple minor detours, but now they were on their way. Any second he would have the honor of welcoming them. Denise's Machine had been tested and retested for the thousandth time. It worked perfectly. Now it waited in the gigantic building behind him for her arrival. And, across the river, on the other side of Biiq, Olga, the kingdom's computer, was humming with life, waiting for Josh.

Everything was set. Now all he had to do was greet them and escort them safely to their destinations. A simple task even for Bud. Well, at least that's what he hoped.

"*Pssst . . . psssssssst.*"

Bud turned and glanced backstage. There he saw the most beautiful creature he had ever laid eyes on. Scientifically, she was perfect. Every part of her was a perfect mathematical ratio to the other—from the length of her arms to the diameter of her knee caps to the width of her toenails. The lady wasn't necessarily pretty, but to a mathematician she was more breathtaking than any unified theory equation.

The Machine

"Most important and excellent of all scientists?" Even her voice vibrated in perfect mathematical frequencies. "Please, if you would be so kind as to tell me where I might find the Machine—the one you've prepared for the female Upside Downer? I have a gift for her."

"Cl-cl-cl-click cl-click CLICK cl-click," Bud stuttered as he left the microphone and approached her. The woman's perfection was definitely fogging his mind.

She frowned slightly, not understanding the clicks.

Realizing she wasn't from Biiq, he nervously fumbled for the translator attached to his belt. He turned it on and repeated himself. It translated his clicks perfectly. Well, almost perfectly. There seemed to be a slight short in the circuits which made it occasionally repeat a word or two. Then there was the problem of Bud's stuttering. . . .

"I'm s-s-sorry s-s-sorry, but that's a s-s-secret s-s-secret," he said. "We have word that the Illusionist has s-s-stolen into our kingdom and is is is trying t-t-to destroy her her."

"The *who*?"

"S-some s-s-sort of ugly queen queen who c-c-can transform her looks looks into any any creature she wants."

"But what of my gift?" the lady asked, managing to smile, flirt, and pout all at the same time.

Bud was mesmerized. Her perfection had captured his heart.

"Surely the most important scientist in the kingdom could figure out something . . . hmm?" She batted her perfectly proportioned eyelids, each with the perfect number of eyelashes.

"D-d-don't worry worry," Bud volunteered, suddenly sounding very gallant. "I'll s-s-ee to it that she g-gets it it personally."

"Oh, thank you, sir." The lady smiled sweetly as she reached out to touch his arm. "You're as kind a man as you are important."

That cinched it. Bud was in love. No doubt about it. He gave a polite little bow as he took the gift into his hands. Then excusing himself (after all, he was an important scientist who had important science-type things to do), he headed back on stage to the microphone. It was then he spotted it—a tiny hole in the bottom corner of the wrapped gift. He turned back to the lady but she was already gone.

That's odd, he thought. *Where could she be?* He glanced about but she was nowhere to be found. *Oh well*, he figured, waving off a pesky fly that had suddenly started buzzing the gift, *she's sure to be in the audience admiring my importance. I'll see her then. Maybe give her a little smile to make her day.* With a confident grin, Bud turned toward the microphone. Again, he noticed the fly. It had landed on the gift and was crawling for the tiny hole. He was about to shoo it away when suddenly . . .

BEEP!........BOP!........BLEEP!.......BURP!....

. . . Listro Q, Aristophenix, and the two Upside Downers made their grand and long-awaited entrance into Biiq. It would have been a bit more grand if Listro Q had not missed his coordinates. Instead of landing on the stage, they landed in a nearby oak tree. Even that wouldn't have been so bad if they had landed right side up. But there they were, all four of them hanging upside down in the giant oak, trying their best to look like proper and distinguished visitors.

"Nice work," Aristophenix muttered between clenched teeth while pretending to smile for the crowd.

"Cool," Listro Q answered as he pretended to look cool for the crowd.

The girl, on the other hand, wasn't interested in pretending anything for the crowd. "Listro Q!" she shouted. "*Listro Q!*"

The Machine

But, before Listro Q had a chance to answer, Bud began his written speech. "sgniteerG sgniteerg, tsom devoleb edispU srenwoD srenwoD." He glanced up from the speech and smiled. But no one was smiling back. In fact, everyone looked pretty confused—as if they didn't understand a word he was saying. What was wrong? What was going on?

He glanced down at the translator attached to his belt. Of course! It was shorting out again. Only worse. Now it wasn't just repeating itself, it was also translating backwards! "diputS diputs, doog rof gnihton, on dnarb eman rotalsnarT," he grumbled before giving it a good thwack with his hand. That did the trick. The backwards problem immediately cleared up. Bud grinned, pleased that all those years in electronics school had finally paid off.

He started again. "Greetings greetings, most beloved Upside Downers Downers. It is with great pleasure pleasure that we welcome you to to the Kingdom of Biiq Biiq—the kingdom of Math Math and Science."

The audience clapped and clicked enthusiastically . . . in perfect mathematical unison, of course.

And so it continued as Bud introduced the governor, the vice-governor, the mayor, the superintendent of transportation, the assistant superintendent of commerce, and on and on—each and every one of them excited to meet the two Upside Downers, and each and every one of them boring the children to death. Bud could see the weariness fill their faces, and he tried his best to hurry through the ceremony. Finally, just a mere four hours, twenty-three minutes, and eight seconds later, the last speech was made and the last hand shaken. The official welcoming was over.

Now, at last, he could take them to his beloved Machine.

⊡

47

"This thing is huge!" Denise exclaimed as they arrived at the giant six-story building. There were no doors, no windows, just walls of smooth, shiny metal. "How do we get in?" she asked.

Bud smiled and produced a skeleton key. He placed it into a nearly invisible lock and gave it a turn. A large door suddenly appeared in the wall, humming to life as it automatically swung open.

"Nice," Denise exclaimed. She threw a look over at Josh. His mouth was dropping open. Not because of the door. But because of what was inside . . .

Before them stretched the biggest laboratory Denise had ever seen. Besides the obligatory bubbling beakers and smoking test tubes, there were thousands of electronic thingamajigs and doohickeys that glowed and flashed everywhere she looked. Some towered several stories over their heads; others stretched hundreds of yards into the distance. But no matter how tall they rose or how far they stretched, and no matter how many different colored lights flashed on how many different panels, they all surrounded and focused upon one thing. . . .

It lay ahead of them in the center of the building. As they approached, it reminded Denise of a large round table. But it didn't seem to have any legs or support of any kind. Instead, it simply floated about waist high. Yet the closer they got, the more she saw it was definitely no table. It was more like a round, floating platform. It consisted of two layers. The bottom layer looked like compacted sand and was about a foot deep. The second layer was a little thinner. It was clear liquid, but a liquid that glowed—almost as brightly as the Center. All around the platform's side, some sort of energy field buzzed and hummed. And high above it hovered a giant, circular TV screen with a single microphone hanging down.

"What . . . is it?" Denise asked in a hushed tone as they arrived.

The Machine

"The experiment experiment," Bud said. He was grinning from ear to ear, obviously filled with pride.

"For what?"

"For you you."

Denise turned to him in surprise. "What?"

"The only way to clearly clearly understand Imager's compassion is to clearly understand his heart heart."

"Yeah, so?"

"So, with this experiment, you will will become a creator. You will gain gain a creator's heart."

Denise looked at him as if he'd lost his mind.

Aristophenix smiled and tried to explain,

**What better way
Imager's love to understand,
than to create your own life form,
to hold in your hand.**

Denise still didn't get it. "What are you guys talking about?"

"Denny?" It was Josh. "I think I understand. These guys have set it all up so you can create a life form." He turned to Bud. "Is that right?"

"Correct correct," Bud agreed.

"And by doing this, they hope you'll experience the same feelings that this Imager supposedly has toward his creation."

"Correct correct again."

"You're not serious?" Denise asked.

"Oh, yes yes, very serious."

"But . . . but I don't know beans about science. I can't just go and create life."

"Don't feel bad," Bud chuckled. "Nobody else has had much much luck in that department, either."

"Then how—"

"Imager. His Breath has already been programmed into the Machine."

"What machine?"

"Why, this whole whole laboratory. We've spent the last three and a half epochs building it for you."

Denise stared, amazed. "For me? You built all this for me?"

Bud nodded. "At Imager's request."

"But . . . how do I . . . I mean, where . . ."

"Don't worry." Bud laughed. "Your only concern is this this platform in front of you . . . and this screen and microphone above you."

"But, I still don't . . ."

"All you have to do is speak speak into the microphone. No matter what you say, great or small small, the Machine will translate your words into action. The Machine will create everything you say within that liquid light. And you will will see what you create on the screen above you."

"This is crazy!" Denise protested.

"No," Listro Q quietly corrected. "Imager's love is this."

She turned to him. "You knew about this?"

Listro Q nodded with a gentle smile. "From our meeting, the very first."

"If you need need any help," Bud said as he turned and prepared to leave, "just tell tell the Machine, and we'll immediately return."

"Wait a minute!" Denise cried in a panic. "You're not leaving me!"

"Yes yes. It's important that you do this this on your own. No one must interfere with what you do do . . . and more importantly no one must interfere with what what you feel."

The Machine

"But I'm sticking around, right?" Josh asked.

"Sorry," Bud answered.

"But *I'm* the one interested in science. *I'm* the one you were going to give a rational explanation for—"

"This isn't about the mind mind, Joshua. This is about the heart."

"Yeah, but—"

"Your studies of logic are with with Olga."

"Who?"

"Our computer—the best in the kingdom."

Josh frowned. It was clear he didn't think a question-and-answer session with some computer rated with creating your very own life-form.

Noticing his obvious disappointment, Listro Q spoke. "Worry don't. For your best will be Olga."

Bud turned back to Denise. "Call us us whenever you want to quit quit or have finished finished. Anytime, day day or night."

"Day or night! It's going to last that long?"

Bud smiled. "That's up up to you."

Denise looked at the platform with its liquid light floating on top of the sand, then up to the Machine surrounding her on all sides. This was insane! And yet, if it really was designed for her, and if it really was safe, and if she really could quit anytime she wanted . . .

On the other hand, all she had was their word. . . .

On the other hand, Josh would kill for this opportunity, so why was she dragging her feet?

On the other hand . . . no, there were too many hands already. It was time for a decision. She turned to Aristophenix, who gave the slightest nod, assuring her everything was okay.

**Don't be a-worryin';
there's nothin' to fear.
To the heart of his feelings,
this will help you draw near.**

Next, she turned to Josh. Good ol' Josh. He'd tell her if it was safe or not.

"Well, kiddo." He flashed her that world-famous grin of his. She could tell he was still envious, but that he was trying to be grown-up about it. "I'm guessing this makes you about the luckiest person I've ever met."

She tried to smile back. This was obviously a new definition of lucky. She wanted to tell him how terrified she was of the whole idea—especially the part of being left alone. But the excitement in his eyes made her feel like some little kid afraid of the dark.

"No one's ever had a chance like this," he said. "And I doubt anyone ever will again."

Denise knew his words were meant to encourage her, that she should be grateful for such an honor. And maybe she should. After all, Josh was right, no one had ever had a chance like this. And it was true, no one probably ever would again. So how could she refuse? And if she did, how could she ever look at herself in the mirror again? Or look at Josh?

She finally had her answer—not because it was what she wanted, but because it was what she *should* want. She turned back to Bud and in her best, I-can-handle-anything tone said, "So when do I start?"

"Right away!" Bud grinned.

Denise swallowed.

"Atta girl," Aristophenix said, slapping her on the back. "It's gonna be great!"

The Machine

"Oh, here here, I'd almost forgotten." Bud reached out and handed Denise the gift he had been carrying under his arm. "It came from a most extraordinary lady lady who wanted to make sure sure you got it."

Denise took the present but paid little attention. At the moment she had a few other things on her mind.

After more "good lucks" and a few hugs, the group finally turned and started for the door. Denise followed them. It wasn't until they were about to step outside that she was again struck with panic. "Joshua!" she cried.

He stopped and turned to her.

She swallowed hard and shook her head. She would be strong. Even if it killed her, she wouldn't admit being afraid—especially to Josh.

He flashed her another grin. "Have fun, kiddo," he said. "What I would give to be in your shoes!"

Denise smiled back, desperately wishing he was.

He turned and joined the others at the door. Everyone waved and gave a few more encouragements.

Denise nodded and waved back.

Bud turned and immediately ran into the side of the door. "Oooh, ouch, ouch!" he cried, grabbing his foot and doing a little jig. "I hate it it when that happens!"

Denise smiled in spite of herself.

After a couple more hops and a few more "ouches," Bud pressed a button inside the building. The door hummed as it started to close. He stepped outside with the others and gave a final wave. A moment later the door shut with a foreboding *boom* that echoed back and forth inside the Machine.

Slowly Denise turned to face the experiment. She had never

admitted to being afraid of anything before—and she wasn't about to start now. So, after taking a deep breath, she started toward the platform of liquid light, all alone in the giant building.

Well, *almost* all alone . . .

Chapter Seven

The Experiment Begins . . .

Denise stood beside the platform of liquid light, more than a little puzzled. Creating your own life-forms was a lot harder than she imagined. Actually creating them wasn't so hard—all she had to do was think something up, say it, and the Machine did the rest. But thinking it up, that was the brain-bruising part.

At first she tried the obvious choices. In front of her was a world of liquid, so she raised her head toward the microphone and called out . . .

"Machine, give me fish."

There was a surge of energy, some flashes and crackles, and she got . . . fish. Billions of them. And from what she could see on the screen above her, there were thousands of different varieties, which was nice . . . for a while.

But, let's face it, they were just fish. It's not like she could have some great, personal relationship with them.

Next she tried animals. You name it, she created it: lions, hippos, giraffes, aardvarks (though she had no great urge to create the smaller, creepy-crawly varieties).

Again, this was nice, but like any great zoo, you can only stand around gawking at the critters so long before you want a little interaction. And since she couldn't get down in the liquid and play with them, they really didn't hold her interest that long.

Then, at last, she had it. . . . People! Like herself. Of course! If she could create people like herself, then she'd have somebody to talk with, to relate to, to be friends with.

"Machine," she said. "Create a me."

The Machine hummed a little louder, the outside energy field sparked a little brighter, until Denise saw an exact duplicate of herself up on the screen. Only, well, not to complain but . . .

It was *too* exact.

Every time Denise moved, it moved. Every time Denise had a thought, it had the same thought.

"This is no fun," Denise muttered.

"This is no fun," the copy of Denise agreed.

"What can we do different?" Denise asked.

"What *can* we do different?" her copy repeated.

"Don't you have any ideas?" Denise asked.

"Don't *you*?" the copy replied.

In many ways it was worse than the fish or animals. How could she be friends with her own reflection? It was like having a computer or a robot who, although it appeared human, thought and felt exactly like she thought and felt. If she said, "I love you," the reply from her other self would be "I love you." If she said, "You're cool," she knew she'd get the same response. It was more like talking into a mirror or a tape recorder than having a real friend.

There had to be another solution. . . .

And then she had it. "Of course, why didn't I think of it before?"

"Of course, why didn't *I*?" came the reply.

Ignoring herself, Denise raised her head to the microphone and ordered, "Machine . . . make a me, that's me but not me!"

Once again the Machine hummed and sparked and flashed. Denise leaned over the platform, waiting breathlessly. She looked up at the screen in anticipation.

And then, at last, her greatest and best creation of all formed inside the liquid light. . . .

The Experiment Begins . . .

Nearly twelve hours had passed before the Illusionist woke up, stretched her six hairy legs, and quietly crept out of the hole at the corner of the gift box. True, the nap might have been a bit longer than necessary, but even the most hideous creature in twenty-three dimensions needed her beauty rest. Besides, she figured destroying Denise would be easy. Since they were alone together inside the Machine, it would be a piece of cake . . . which, now that she was in the form of a fly, sounded pretty appealing—especially the frosting part.

It wasn't that the Illusionist hated Denise. It was that Imager loved her. And since the Illusionist hated Imager, and since the best way to hurt someone you hate is to destroy someone they love . . . well, the Illusionist really didn't have any choice in the matter. She *had* to destroy Denise.

But instead of going immediately for the kill, the Illusionist decided to remain disguised as a fly just a little bit longer. That way she could buzz the Machine a few times to check it out and see what the big deal was. Even in her part of the universe, the Illusionist had heard plenty about this newfangled invention that was being built, and how Imager hoped to instruct an Upside Downer with it.

Soon, she was airborne. And looking down upon Denise and the glowing platform, the Illusionist grew sick to her stomach. She was not prepared to see such innocence and goodness, such sweetness and kindness. It was absolutely disgusting, thoroughly nauseating.

But that was okay because it would soon come to an end. Very, very soon it would all be over . . .

After Denise created her latest and best creation, she decided to make two of them. After all, the only thing better than playing with one person was to play with two. She suspected she would create more than that in the future, but right now two was enough—two little life-forms in liquid light, splashing, playing, and joking with each other and with her.

She called them *Gus* and *Gertrude*. She wasn't sure why; the names just seemed to fit.

Physically, they looked exactly like Denise—well, except for the extra set of arms. Denise always thought that human-types were a little shortchanged in that department, and she wanted her creations to have every advantage. "This way you can brush your teeth and comb your hair at the same time," she explained.

Of course they couldn't see Denise. She was too big. In fact, she was so big that they just figured she was everywhere. In a sense, they were right. But even though they couldn't see her, they could hear her. That was one of the orders Denise had given to the Machine. And it was one of her best. Now the three of them could talk and joke and laugh for as long as they wanted.

Gus was the funniest—all huffy and puffy and pretending to have all the answers when most of the time he didn't have a clue. How could he? He was only a few hours old! But that didn't stop him from trying.

Gertie (she made it clear from the start that she hated the name Gertrude) was also a crack-up. The little gal could get so excited over the simplest things. "Look, everybody! I have a toe! I have a toe! And I can wiggle it!" And when she wasn't getting excited about having toes or fingers or a belly button, she was constantly bombarding Denise with a thousand *whys*, *what ifs*, and *how comes*?

They were incredibly cute, reminding Denise of a couple pup-

The Experiment Begins . . .

pies, the way they romped and climbed and played over each other. Better yet, they reminded her of baby-sitting the Jefferson twins (when they were on their *best* behavior and when they *didn't* need their diapers changed).

But it was more than just their cuteness and playfulness. There was something else. Denise couldn't put her finger on it, but she'd never felt anything quite like it before. As she continued to watch them, her chest began to ache. But it wasn't a bad ache, it was an ache of pleasure—in fact sometimes there was so much pleasure that it was hard for her to breathe. And the more she hovered over her creations, watching and encouraging them in their new adventure called *life*, the more wonderful the ache grew. Whatever this feeling was, it was safe to say that Denise was definitely becoming attached to these little folks.

And they were becoming attached to her. In fact, Gertie put it best when Denise had to leave for a bathroom break. She was gone only a few minutes, but when she returned Gertie had her arms folded (all four of them) and began to scold Denise for being gone so long. "It was awful," she complained in her cute little high-pitched voice. "It was like a part of me was missing. Don't you ever ever *ever* do that again!"

"Okay, okay," Denise chuckled. "I promise I won't ever *ever* ever do that again." But even as she joked with her, Denise knew Gertie was right. She *was* a part of them. And they were a part of *her*. And why not? After all, didn't they come from Denise's own personality and imagination? Gus with his know-it-all, I'll-tackle-the-world mentality, and cute little Gertie with all of her questions and that big, sensitive heart of hers. Both were definitely a part of Denise . . . and she was definitely a part of them.

Then it happened.

"Hey, guys!" Gus shouted. "Watch this!"

He was showing off by swimming little figure eights in the liquid light. Denise looked down at the ripples on the platform. As he swam faster, the figure eights grew bigger and the waves grew taller. It was pretty impressive, even to Denise.

Gertie had floated to the surface to get a better view, and as Gus kept making bigger waves, she kept bobbing up and down, higher and lower. "*Whoa, whoo, wee* . . . okay, Gus," she cried between bobs, "cut it *ow, wow, woooo* . . . I'm not kidding now, stop, *eeeee, ooh*."

Soon Denise and Gertie were laughing so hard that tears streamed down their cheeks. But not Gus. He was really getting into it. And as his figure eights grew larger and larger, he began swimming closer and closer to the platform's edge.

"Okay, Gus," Denise finally called out through her laughter. "That's enough now."

But Gus didn't hear.

Denise called a little louder, "Okay, Gus."

By now he was much closer to the edge . . . too close. And he still wasn't paying attention.

"Gus . . . Gus!"

No answer.

Denise fought back the rising panic inside her. Any second he could swim out too far; any second he could accidentally swim over the edge and fall to his death.

"*Gus!*" she shouted.

Gertie joined in. "Gus!" she cried. "Gus!"

But there was still no response.

Denise's panic turned to cold fear as Gus started the next figure eight—his biggest one yet—the one taking him straight toward the edge. What could she do? How could she stop him?

The Experiment Begins . . .

"GUS . . . GUS, LISTEN TO ME . . . GUS!"

But Gus didn't hear.

Suddenly a thought came to Denise. As a last-ditch effort she quickly turned to the microphone and shouted, "Machine, create a wall!"

The Machine hummed and immediately a wall sprang up around the edge of the platform. And just in time! It had barely formed before Gus hit it . . . head on. It was close, but Denise had managed to save Gus just before he'd have fallen over the edge to his death.

Yet, instead of showing his appreciation, Gus glared up at the sky, rubbing his head. "Hey!" he shouted. "What do you think you're doing?"

"You were swimming off the edge," Denise explained. "I had to stop you with this wall."

"What do you mean *edge*, what's an *edge*?"

"It's, uh . . . an ending . . ."

"An ending?"

"Yeah, it's a . . ." But try as she might, Denise couldn't find a word he'd understand. "It's something that would kill you," she explained.

"Kill?"

"You would stop living and thinking. You'd stop . . . existing."

"Go on!" Gus shouted.

"No, I'm serious."

Gus was still angry and still rubbing his head. "So why didn't you tell me? This wall thing of yours packs a pretty big wallop."

"She tried to tell you," Gertie called. "She shouted at you over and over again."

"I didn't hear a thing. Just the roar."

"The roar?" Denise asked.

"Yeah, a roar that kept getting louder and louder."

Denise threw a glance at the edge of the platform. "Oh that . . . that's the energy field all around the platform. I think it holds it together. I guess it just drowned me out."

"What do you mean, *energy field*?" Gus asked.

"And what's a *platform*?" Gertie wondered. "And what do you mean, *drowned*? And what—"

"Never mind," Denise laughed, relieved that they were back to asking questions, "never mind. Let's just say it's a good idea not to get so close to the edge."

"You're not kidding," Gus agreed. "That wall of yours is no treat, and this *kill* stuff doesn't sound so hot either. Thanks for the warning."

"No problem." Denise smiled.

◘

But she wouldn't have been smiling if she had known what the Illusionist was thinking. By circling high overhead the creature had seen everything. Everything from the sickening friendship and love between Denise and the creatures . . . to Gus's near-destruction by swimming too close to the edge.

And, as she watched, a plan started to form. It was one thing to simply destroy Denise. But it was quite another to make her writhe and suffer in agony first. The Illusionist broke into a grin. *Writhing* and *suffering* . . . two of her favorite words.

Without a moment's hesitation, the Illusionist folded her wings back and dove straight for the platform. Then just before she splashed into the liquid light, she transformed herself into the shape of Gus and Gertie—complete with the four arms.

◘

Across the river, on the other side of Biiq, Josh stood in front of another type of machine . . . Olga. She was no taller than a boy and no thicker than, say, your average, run-of-the-mill breakfast waffle (complete, of course, with all those little square holes). Like a giant fence, Olga snaked in and around the entire kingdom. She circled houses and buildings, she passed under overpasses and over underpasses, she cut through farmer's fields, and she crossed over streams—around and around and back and forth she wound as far as the eye could see.

"What is it?" Josh asked.

"She's one of the most powerful computers in our dimension." Bud grinned. "We use her to explore and better understand Imager."

Josh took a deep breath. He wanted to be liked by the folks, but all this talk about Imager was starting to get to him. "Look," he said politely. "I appreciate what you're trying to do. But there's just no way you can scientifically prove there's some sort of . . . *Supreme Being* out there—someone who knows all and sees all."

Bud started to speak, but Josh wasn't finished. "I'm not saying there isn't *something*. I mean I definitely experienced things at the Center. But like I told the Weaver, to try and prove it scientifically . . . I'm sorry, it's just not possible."

Bud traded smiles with Aristophenix and Listro Q. Then he reached over and pressed a single button on the computer. Immediately a thin sheet of water shot from Olga and floated before them. It was about three feet long and a foot wide.

Josh was impressed.

"It's only a projected image," Bud said. "See?" He ran his hands through it. "Just like a holograph."

Josh reached out and touched the water. It was true. There was nothing there. It was just a picture of water floating in midair.

"Tell me me," Bud asked. "What do you know about geometry?"

"A little. We haven't had it at school yet or anything, but I've done some reading."

"Good good. In the Upside-Down Kingdom, how many many dimensions do you live in in?"

"Three," Josh answered. "In our world we have three dimensions. Everything has length, that's one dimension—and width, that's two dimensions—and height, that's the third. Everything from a penny to a skyscraper has three dimensions."

"Very good. But what if there were more than three dimensions?"

"Some scientists think time is a fourth dimension."

Bud couldn't help smiling. "Interesting theory. But could five, six, or seven dimensions also exist? Is that that possible?"

"Mathematically, sure. But we could never see them—they'd be past our understanding."

"Precisely."

"Hold it, wait a minute. Are you saying this Imager guy lives in a dimension higher than ours?"

"The highest."

"But . . . if that's true, well, you could never prove him."

"Yes and no," Bud answered. "The only way to understand higher dimensions is to use the dimensions we already have."

Josh looked at him, waiting for more.

"Let's pretend this sheet of water floating in front of us us has only two dimensions. It has length"—he ran his finger across the longer side of the projection—"and it has width." He motioned to the shorter side. "But it it has no height, no tallness. In other words, let's say there's a sideways and a back-and-forth, but no up-and-down."

Josh nodded.

"Now let's let's pretend there are people living in in this two-dimensional world—a world completely flat. They would under-

64

stand back-and-forth and sideways, but they would have no understanding of up-and-down, correct?"

Again Josh nodded.

"How how would we in the the next higher dimension, in the third dimension, appear to them?"

"If they looked up they'd see us like giants staring down at them," Josh said.

"No . . . they wouldn't know how to look look up. Remember, they have no up-and-down . . . all they they have in their two-dimensional world is back-and-forth and sideways."

"Well, then, I guess . . . they'd never be able to see us at all."

"Precisely. Does that mean mean we wouldn't be here?"

"No, we'd be here. And we could see everything about them, all the time . . . from one end of this projection to the other . . . we could see their whole life."

"And if we wanted them to see see us, what would we do?"

"I guess we'd have to get down to their level." Josh began to chuckle. "It would sure be a shock to them, though." He reached toward the floating projection. "I mean, it would be like, *poof*"— he stuck his fingertip into the image—"we'd suddenly appear, then *poof*"—he pulled out his finger—"we'd suddenly disappear."

"But would we really disappear?"

"No . . . like I said, we'd be there all the time. But to them, we'd be like these . . . these . . . " Josh came to a stop. The thought boggled his mind. He looked up at Bud, his eyes growing wide with understanding.

"To them what would we be like like, Josh?" Bud gently asked.

After a moment Josh slowly spoke the words. "To them we'd be like . . . we'd be all-knowing, all-seeing." Josh swallowed hard. Then after another pause, he concluded, "To them we'd be like . . . God."

Chapter Eight

Choices

Dozing off was the last thing Denise had in mind, particularly after Gertie's lecture about leaving them. But after a day of school, traveling across dimensions, visiting the Center, nearly seeing Imager, ceasing to exist, being rewoven, the endless welcome ceremony, and all the hours of fun with Gus and Gertie, well, she didn't have much choice. She was just going to lie down for a second to rest her eyes. Unfortunately, that second turned into nearly an hour.

And an Illusionist can do a lot of damage in nearly an hour.

The first thing Denise noticed when she woke up and looked at the platform was that the wall she created had a hole in it. How odd.

The second thing she noticed was that on the other side of the wall, just a hair's breadth from the edge, were Gus's waves!

"Gus?" she cried as she raced to the platform. "Get away from the edge! Gus, what are you doing?"

But Gus couldn't hear her. He was too close to the edge. The roar was too loud.

Desperation gripped Denise. Any second Gus could lose his balance. Any second he could fall onto the floor and be destroyed! What could she do, what could be done?

Then she remembered . . . the Machine!

She spun to the microphone and yelled, "Machine! Pick up Gus and put him back into the center of—"

"Not so fast, dear heart."

The voice sent a chill through Denise. She recognized it at once. She had heard it a dozen times in her dreams. She had heard

Choices

it high over the trees of Keygarp. But now . . . now it came from somewhere on the platform!

"What are you doing here?" Denise shouted. She tried to push back the fear, as she searched for a telltale ripple in the liquid light. "Where are you?"

"I'm right here."

"Where?" Denise demanded.

"Why, with Gertie, of course."

Denise stifled a gasp. *The Illusionist—with Gertie*? "Machine!" she cried. "Show me Gertie!"

Immediately Gertie's image flickered onto the screen overhead. Beside her was another creature who looked almost identical to her. The chill Denise had felt earlier grew to a cold numbness. This other creation was *not* hers.

"Hi, Denny," Gertie's voice called cheerfully.

"Hi, Gertie," Denise answered. Her eyes desperately searched the platform for their location. There! She spotted them! Two tiny ripples near the center. She continued talking, trying to keep her voice calm and steady. Whatever was happening, she didn't want to scare her sensitive little friend. "What's going on, Gertie? What's Gus doing?"

"Oh, he's just exercising his free will."

"His what?"

"The lady here explained it all to us," Gertie chirped. "If Gus wants to play at the edge, he has every right to."

"That's right," the Illusionist agreed. Her voice was smooth and seductive. "Otherwise you'd be living in a prison, wouldn't you?"

"Uh-huh," Gertie said, "and Denny wouldn't want that."

"No, of course she wouldn't," the Illusionist said. "Because Denny loves you, doesn't she?"

Gertie agreed, "With her whole heart."

Suddenly there was a piercing scream. "*Ahhhh . . .*"

Denise spun back to the edge of the platform. The little ripples that had surrounded Gus were gone. Instead, there was just a pinpoint glimmer of reflection falling from the platform.

It was Gus!

Without thinking, Denise dove toward the glimmer—arm outstretched, hand open. It was close, but just before she hit the floor, she felt the faintest tickle inside her palm. Gus had landed safely in her open hand.

"Wooo-eeee!" he shouted as Denise rolled onto her back and struggled to her feet. "That was somethin'! Hey, Gertie, if you can hear me, you ought to come over and try this!"

"What are you doing?" Denise shouted angrily at him. "You could have killed yourself. Gus . . . *Gus!*"

"It will do no good, dear heart," the Illusionist chuckled. "He can't hear you. You know that—not near the edge."

"Fine, then I'll put him back here in the middle where he—"

"But he doesn't want to be in the middle. He wants to be at the edge."

"I know that, but—"

"She's got a point, Denny." It was Gertie again—just as sweet and thoughtful as ever. "You wouldn't want to make him live someplace he doesn't want to. You want him to have free will, right?"

There was that phrase again. Already Denise was beginning to hate it. For a moment she was tempted to shout, "*I don't care about any stupid free will! I'm the boss and what I say goes!*" But she didn't. Somehow she knew that being a demanding bully wasn't exactly what their friendship was about. So she tried reason. . . .

"Look, I know that's what he wants—to play on the edge. But

68

Choices

I also know it'll kill him. So I have to save him. I have to tell him."

"But you already did," the Illusionist reminded her. "And he chose not to listen."

"But he listened to you just fine, didn't he?" There was no missing the anger growing in Denise's voice.

"I have my ways," the Illusionist chuckled.

"Yeah, well, I have mine, too." With a determined voice Denise turned to the microphone. "Machine, I want you to take this, this stranger here, and I want you to—"

"Hold on, child."

Denise stopped.

"So what are you going to do—destroy me?"

"The thought had crossed my mind."

"That's rich," the Illusionist laughed. "So is that what you do? Destroy anyone who disagrees with you?"

"No, of course she wouldn't." Gertie's little voice was also growing angry at the Illusionist. "Denny isn't that way. Are you, Denny?"

"Well, no . . ." Denise faltered, "of course not."

"See?" Gertie challenged. "Denny loves us."

"Love," the Illusionist sneered. "You call this love? Making people live where they don't want to live . . . destroying those who don't agree with her? That is not love."

Once again the tops of Denise's ears started to burn. She'd had enough talk. Now it was time for action. "Machine," she shouted, "I want you to take this—this thing and—"

"I guarantee you!" the Illusionist shouted over her.

In spite of herself, Denise came to a stop.

"If you destroy me, I guarantee that Gus and Gertie will never love you on their own. They'll only pretend to love you. They'll be afraid that if they don't, you'll destroy them just as you did me!"

Denise's head began to swim. She knew there was some truth to the Illusionist's words. She also knew that she wanted to completely wipe the creature off the face of the platform. And if those weren't enough emotions raging inside her, there was also her worry about Gus.

"Why . . ." She turned back to the Illusionist, the feelings tightening her throat. "Why are you doing this to us? Things were so good before. Everything was so perfect."

"Since when is a dictatorship perfect?" the Illusionist demanded.

"But I'm no dictator, I'm . . . I'm—"

"Hey, are you going to put me down or what!" Gus demanded. Denise looked back into her palm.

"Put me on the edge, put me on the edge!" he shouted. "I want to jump off again, I want to jump off!"

Denise stared into her hand, angry at the tears welling up in her eyes. "Gus," she stammered, "don't you see? It will kill you."

But he didn't hear. "Put me down! I want to jump off again! I want to jump off!"

"Gus . . . please . . ." By now the tears were forming faster than Denise could blink them away. "Please, listen to me. Gus . . ."

"Cry all you want," the Illusionist taunted, "but he won't hear you. It was his choice to go to the edge. Now he will *never* hear you!"

The words cut deeply into Denise. One of her closest and best friends was trying to kill himself. No, he was more than a best friend. He was a part of her. A part of her was trying to kill himself . . . and there seemed little she could do to stop him.

"Gus . . . ," she croaked hoarsely, "please . . ."

But there was no answer except, "Put me down, put me down! I want to jump off again! I want to jump off!"

Choices

"Isn't there . . ." She looked back at the platform where the Illusionist was, hoping for some way out, *any* way out. "Isn't there *something* I can do?"

"Not a thing," the Illusionist smiled.

Denise looked back at her palm.

"Put me down! I want to jump off! I want to jump off!"

She stood a long moment, listening, thinking. . . .

The Illusionist was right: Denise could demand that Gus stay in the middle, but then she'd be a dictator. She could build an impossibly thick wall around him, but then she'd be a prison guard. She could wipe out the Illusionist, but then she'd be a murderer.

The realization pressed heavily upon Denise's chest, making it difficult to breathe. The knot in her throat continued to tighten. But there was nothing she could do. She saw that now.

"Gus . . . please?"

"Put me down! Put me down!"

Denise remained listening to his demands, her mind racing, probing every possibility. But there was no way out.

"Gus . . . ," she pleaded one final time.

But his answer was the same.

Then, her heart aching, Denise lowered her hand back toward the edge of the platform. "Good-bye," she whispered softly. "Good-bye, my friend."

"Put me down! Put me down!"

"Good-bye . . ."

He leaped from her palm and she saw the ripples as he landed back in the liquid light.

"Don't worry, Denny."

She looked back to the monitor and saw Gertie. Her little friend was also crying.

"You still have me," Gertie sniffed. "And I'll never leave you. I promise I'll never, never leave you."

Denise tried to smile. Good ol' Gertie. Always the sensitive, bighearted Gertie. But wait! Suddenly a thought came to mind. Of course, why hadn't she thought of it before? It was a long shot. But maybe . . .

"*Eeee-yaaaa* . . ." Once again Gus had raced to the edge of the platform and was leaping off.

Immediately Denise slid her hand underneath the edge and caught him.

"What are you doing?" the Illusionist yelled. "You're depriving him of his free will!"

But Denise paid no attention. "Gertie!" she called. "Gertie, will you do me a favor?"

"Of course, Denny, whatever you want."

"Will you give a message to Gus?"

"Now wait a minute," the Illusionist protested. "That's not fair."

"Of course it's fair!" Denise grinned, wiping away the tears with her free hand. "He may not be able to hear me, but there's nothing saying I can't write him a note."

"Put me down!" Gus shouted from inside her palm. "Put me down!"

"Unfair!" the Illusionist shouted. Her voice grew shriller. "Unfair!"

But Denise no longer listened. "Machine," she commanded. "Write a message. Put it on something that will last and see to it that Gertie gets it."

The Machine hummed a brief moment in preparation and awaited further orders.

"This is unfair!" the Illusionist continued to shout. "Stop it at once!"

Choices

"Put me down! Put me down!" Gus kept demanding.

But Denise wasn't stopping for anyone. She'd found the solution. Speaking to the Machine, she ordered, "Have the message read: *Do not jump off the edge—it will kill you!*"

The Machine gave a faint crackle. Suddenly there was another ripple in the liquid light. Denise looked up to the monitor to see a large steel sign appear close to Gertie.

It was more than the Illusionist could bear. As quickly as the sign appeared, she disappeared. One minute she was there, the next minute she was gone. Denise had no idea where she went and hoped never to see her again.

But, even now, she had her doubts . . .

Chapter Nine

The Sign

"Oh, look," Gertie sighed. She slowly drifted toward the gigantic steel sign resting on the floor of her liquid light ocean. "It's so . . . so . . . beautiful."

Now the truth is, it really wasn't all that beautiful—just an ordinary sign with a message engraved on it. But the fact that it came from her creator, that it came from her Denny, well, that brought tears of gratitude to young Gertie's eyes. "Thank you *soo* much," she kept repeating over and over again. "Thank you so very much."

Denise was deeply touched. It seemed the tiniest of things brought joy to Gertie. And somehow that made Denise love her all the more.

"You're so beautiful," Gertie exclaimed, as she tenderly reached out to touch the sign. "And your letters . . . they're carved so perfectly."

For a moment Denise was confused. Who was Gertie talking to? Then realizing Gertie wasn't addressing her but the sign, Denise politely cleared her throat. "Ah, Gertie . . . Gertie, it's me, Denny. I'm still up here."

"Oh, sorry." Gertie gave an embarrassed giggle as she glanced up to the sky. "I knew that."

Denise smiled. "Now, listen, I need you to take that message to—"

"Put me down, put me down!" It was Gus. He was still in her palm. She lowered her hand and let him jump back onto the edge of the platform. She quickly turned to Gertie, who had already resumed her conversation.

"Wonderful sign . . . perfect sign."

The Sign

"Gertie?"

"Your letters say such truth, such—"

"Gertie . . ."

But Gertie was so busy admiring the sign that she barely heard.

"*Gertie!*"

That did the trick. "Oh . . . uh, hi, Denny." But even as she answered, she sounded a little confused, a little distracted. "What were we talking about?"

"Will you ask Gus to read this sign?"

"Of course I will—I'd love to."

"Thank you," Denise said. "I'll just order the Machine to move it over to him and then you can show him—"

"Oh, no, I can carry it," Gertie volunteered cheerfully.

Denise couldn't help smiling. Once again she was moved by her friend's love and desire to help. But she didn't need her help. "That's okay," Denise answered, "there's no need for you to—"

"No, no, I'd love to carry it for you."

"Thanks, Gertie, but I don't think—"

"You're so beautiful." Gertie's voice grew dreamy again. "Your letters are so perfect, so full of truth . . . I'll carry you everywhere you want to go."

"Gertie, it's just a sign. You're talking to a—"

"I'll carry you anywhere—forever and ever."

"Gertie . . . *Gertie!*"

But Gertie didn't answer. Before Denise could stop her, she took the huge sign into her four hands and, with great effort, heaved it onto her back. It was so heavy that she sank into the sandy ocean floor. It was so big and bulky that it stretched out far over her head. But she forced herself to start walking. The awful weight caused her to groan with every step, but Gertie seemed happy to bear that weight. Honored to bear it. She would do anything for her Denny. Anything.

"Gertie!" Denise felt a twinge of panic. "Gertie, listen to me!"

But Gertie no longer heard. The steel plate that stretched over her head blocked all sound from above.

"Gertie, listen to me!"

Gertie continued to stagger forward, groaning under the weight, deaf to Denise's voice . . . as if she had more important things to do.

"Please, Gertie . . ." Denise could feel the emotion rising to her throat again. Could it be? First she'd lost Gus and now . . . "Gertie! Gertie, listen to me!"

But her voice continued to bounce off the steel plate, never reaching Gertie's ears. Suddenly Denise felt very alone. "You're cutting me off," she called. "Gertie, please . . . don't do this!"

There was no answer.

Gus gave another scream as he jumped from the platform. Again Denise leaped forward to catch him. But again, at his insistence, she put him back on the edge—none too gently this time.

"Hey! Watch it!" he shouted before starting his run toward the edge again.

Denise was lost. Something had to be done. Gertie could never carry that sign—not for long. She wasn't created to carry it. She'd wear herself out. In desperation, Denise turned back to the Machine and gave another order. "Machine . . . another sign!"

The Machine hummed in preparation.

"Have it read: *Listen to me!*"

The Machine gave a faint crackle and immediately the sign appeared in front of Gertie.

But to Denise's horror, Gertie's gruntings and groanings grew twice as loud.

The Sign

Denise looked back to the screen. Instead of obeying the second sign, Gertie had placed it onto her back with the first one!

"No!" Denise shouted.

But she was too late. Now Gertie's burden was doubly hard to carry. Now it was doubly hard for her to hear Denise's warnings.

"Gertie," she cried, "please don't do this to yourself! Please listen to me . . ."

Feeling light-headed from all the emotion, Denise grabbed the edge of the platform for support and looked down to watch Gertie's ripples of light moving slower and slower. The poor thing was obviously wearing herself out. Denise looked back to the screen. The weight was causing her friend to sink further into the sandy bottom. With every step she took, she sank deeper and deeper. Soon, she was waist deep in the sand and still sinking. In a matter of minutes the ocean floor would swallow her. The sand would cover her neck, her mouth, her nose; and then, in her stubborn desire to serve Denise, Gertie would suffocate and kill herself.

"Ahhhh!" Gus screamed as he jumped off the edge.

Denise dove forward and caught him, then returned to Gertie. But Gertie was gone! There were no sounds, no ripples, no image on the screen!

"*Gertie!*"

Desperate, Denise shoved her free hand deep into the liquid light where she had last seen Gertie. It was an impulsive move that could have crushed her little friend, but she had to do something.

At the same time Gus continued his demands, "Put me down, put me down!"

Then Denise heard her. She was coughing up sand and screaming hysterically, but there was no mistaking Gertie's voice. "Let me go, let me go!"

For a moment the tiniest relief filled Denise. But only for a moment.

"Put me down! Put me down!"

"Let me go! Let me go!"

"Stop this!" Denise shouted into both of her hands. "You two are killing yourselves! Don't you see? Stop it!"

But neither was listening.

"Put me down! Let me go!" Their voices were blending into one. "Put me down! Let me go! Put me down! Let me go!"

Then another voice joined in. Denise wasn't sure where it came from, but there was no mistaking who it was. "You must let them go, dear heart, or they will be your prisoners. Without free will, you will become their dictator."

"But they'll kill themselves!" Denise shouted.

"Put me down! Let me go! Put me down! . . ."

Moisture again filled Denise's eyes. She was cut off from both friends now. Friends who were destroying themselves. Her two best friends were destroying themselves, and there was nothing she could do to stop them!

Her throat ached. The pressure inside her chest was so great that she had to fight for breath. "Please, Gus," she begged, "Gertie, please . . . you two have to listen to me!" Her head grew lighter as she struggled for breath. Hot tears spilled from her eyes and ran down her face.

"You need me!" she screamed in anger. "Listen to me! You need me!"

But there was no answer. Only their continual demands—

"Put me down! Let me go! Put me down! Let me go!"

Denise's vision began to blur. The hours without sleep, the intense emotions, and the ongoing fight to save the ones she so deeply loved was more than she could bear.

The Sign

"Please . . . ," she groaned, "please . . ."

But it did no good. By now both Gus and Gertie were in a mindless rage. Gus was the first to add the new phrase. "I hate you!" he shouted. "I hate you! I hate you! Put me down! I hate you!"

Soon Gertie had joined in. "I hate you! Let me go! Let me go! I hate you!"

The words hit Denise hard, slamming into her gut . . . and breaking her heart.

"I hate you! I hate you! I hate you!"

Her head began to reel. She had only fainted once in her life. She hated the feeling then, and she hated it now. She had to fight it off, she knew it. But she also knew something else. She knew the Illusionist was right. She knew there was nothing more she could do for them.

Slowly . . . sadly . . . Denise unclenched one hand. Her mind screamed with anguish as Gus jumped off into the liquid light and swam back to the edge of the platform—for the very last time.

Then, no longer able to see through her tears or to stop the room as it started to spin, Denise opened her other hand. Suddenly she closed it and pulled back, yelling, "No! I can't!"

"Let me go! Let me go!" Gertie screamed.

"Nooo!"

"I hate you! I hate you! Let me go! Let me go!"

"You have no choice, dear heart," the gentle voice cooed. "You know that. No choice . . ."

Denise was weeping now. The Illusionist was right, there was nothing she could do. Once again she opened her hand and slowly brought it toward the platform. Once again the pain pierced her heart as Gertie dove into the liquid light and swam toward her precious signs.

Denise tried to speak, to say something. But as she clung helplessly to the platform, no words would come.

The tears turned to sobs—gulping, gut-wrenching sobs. She had never cried so hard, never felt such anguish. She wasn't just losing friends, she was losing her heart.

It was cold inside the Machine now . . . very cold.

She could no longer stand to watch. The pressure was too great. Hanging onto the edge of the platform, Denise slowly eased herself down to the floor. The sobs continued, only now they were silent sobs—sobs of hopelessness.

She released her grip on the platform and drew herself into a tiny little ball on the cold concrete floor.

The pain was unbearable.

Chapter Ten

Another Last Chance

Across the river with Bud and the guys, Josh was still learning about Imager. He didn't believe everything they said, but gradually, scientific theory by scientific theory, and mathematical formula by mathematical formula, he was beginning to realize there must be *somebody* out there.

"But what about the future?" he asked. "Everybody—you guys, the Weaver, folks at Fayrah, they all say this Imager knows our future, that he knows what I'm going to do before I do."

Aristophenix, Listro Q, and Bud all nodded in agreement.

"But that's impossible!"

"Impossible more, that doesn't he," Listro Q offered.

"How?"

Bud grinned. "It's simple. If you would just just imagine—"

"No imaginings," Josh said firmly. "Your theory about higher dimensions is interesting but that's all it is—theory. I still need proof."

Aristophenix and Listro Q exchanged nervous glances.

But Bud simply smiled and pushed several buttons on Olga. Immediately a long paper slipped out of a slot.

"What's that?"

"Your future future."

"Yeah, right," Josh scoffed.

But Bud was perfectly serious. "Every one of your personality traits is given given a number. See . . ." He held the paper out, but an immediate frown crossed his face. "This is strange strange. All the information seems to be be printed upside down."

Josh looked over Bud's shoulder a moment and then, without a word, gently took the paper from him and turned it right side up.

"Oh, thank you, much better." Bud grinned sheepishly. "Now where where were we?"

"Something about my personality traits having a number?"

"Precisely. See, your athletic abilities are number 706, your interest in science is 245, your desire to please people is—"

"Wait a minute, how do you know all that about me?"

"We know everything about you you."

"*Everything*?"

"Everything," Bud grinned. "Remember, we look down down from a higher dimension."

"Oh, yeah, right." Josh swallowed a little uncomfortably. Suddenly he wasn't so thrilled that everything he did was always watched.

"Anyway," Bud continued, "everything about you is given a number and everything that could happen to you is given given another number. Then, using the laws of probability, we run run these numbers through the computer and it mathematically tells us what you'll do do in every situation."

"What if I want to change my mind?"

"You can change your mind mind as often as you want. But we know what your final decision will be be."

"No kidding?"

"And we can predict how that decision will affect other people people in their mathematical future."

"And if you put all of our mathematical futures together . . ."

"We know the entire future future of your world."

"Incredible."

"No," Bud answered. "Just Imager's mathematics."

"Can I see it?" Josh asked, reaching for the paper.

"No, uh, I don't think so so."

"Why not? It's *my* future."

"According to these figures figures, you would try and alter these numbers."

"No way," Josh protested.

"Yes, you would."

"Absolutely not."

"Just as you didn't try to alter the Weaver's tapestry?"

"Well, that was different."

"How how?"

"Well, because . . . I mean . . ." Josh was running out of arguments. As much as he hated to admit it, Bud had a point. "Well, okay, I guess maybe I might try—just a little."

The group chuckled quietly. Even Josh had to smile. Then an idea came to mind. "What about Denny?" he asked. "Could I see her future?"

Bud glanced at Aristophenix and Listro Q. They hesitated a moment, then nodded.

Bud reached over and pressed another set of Olga buttons. Immediately another long sheet of paper shot out. He picked it up and began showing the figures to Josh. "See, this number here is your friend's stubbornness, this one is her doubt doubt over Imager's love—the reason she came here in the first place."

Josh nodded.

"This one is her love for the creatures she's just just created over at the Machine. And this this . . ." Bud's voice trailed off.

"What?" Josh asked.

"No no, this can't be right." Immediately Bud re-pushed the buttons on the computer and immediately another piece of paper shot out.

"What's wrong?" Josh asked as Bud quickly scanned the paper.

Bud's face grew pale.

"Bud?" Aristophenix asked. There was no missing the concern in his voice. "Bud?"

Finally the scientist spoke, "According to these calculations, Denny is experiencing a love for her creation similar to Imager's."

"Well, that's great!" Josh exclaimed. "I mean, that's what she wanted to understand, right?"

Still staring at the figures Bud could only shake his head. "But too too similar," he quietly murmured.

"Too similar, how?" Listro Q asked. "Similar love, how to Imager?"

Slowly Bud looked up. "Completely," he said. "A love so similar that it would destroy itself to save its creation."

A chill swept over the group.

Then, without a word, Aristophenix quickly turned and started waddling down the path toward the bridge.

"Where are you going?" Josh shouted.

The pudgy creature called over his shoulder,

> Our tooshes should be a-movin',
> 'cause I'm afraid if they don't,
> Denny's chances of livin',
> are less than remote!

⊡

Denise wasn't sure when the idea first came. But there, curled up on the cold floor, she realized she hadn't tried everything. There was still one last thing she could do to try and save her friends.

She struggled to her knees, then rose unsteadily to her feet. A wave of dizziness swept over her, but she wouldn't give in to it.

Another Last Chance

Those were her friends on that platform and nothing would stop her from saving them.

She glanced quickly over to the edge. Gus's ripples were still there. Good. That meant he hadn't jumped off yet. Apparently he enjoyed teetering on the edge as much as he did the actual falling.

She glanced up to the screen for Gertie's location. To her amazement her little friend had already reached the wall. Gertie's fierce determination surprised her. Then again, Gertie was part of her, and if there was one thing Denise had, it was determination. But Gertie was so much weaker now. As with Gus, it was only a short matter of time before she also destroyed herself.

It was an awful risk. Denise didn't even know if the Machine could pull it off—let alone if she'd survive. Then there was the matter of coming back. But it was the only hope Gus and Gertie had. If they wouldn't let her help from above, then maybe, just maybe she could help from beside.

"Machine!" she shouted.

The Machine hummed in readiness.

"Put me in their world! Make me like Gus and Gertie!"

The Machine crackled and sparked longer than normal. This was obviously no common request. At last a beam shot out and struck her, shrinking her to the size of a pinhead. Then, instantly, it transported her into Gus and Gertie's world.

The whole process took less than a minute and it definitely caught her off guard. Shrinking to the size of a pinhead is not your everyday experience. Then there was the matter of swimming and breathing in the liquid light. And finally, let's not forget the four arms. It took lots of concentration not to tangle them up and even more not to accidentally clobber herself with them. But finally she got the hang of it. And just in time.

"Who are you?"

The voice was faint and weak but Denise immediately recognized it. "Gertie?" she cried, desperately searching. "Gertie, where are you?"

"I'm right here," Gertie groaned. "Down here."

Denise looked down to the sandy ocean floor and let out a gasp. By now Gertie had sunk up to her neck. Yet she still hung onto the heavy signs—holding them high over her head. Nothing would make her let go.

"Quick, let me have those," Denise shouted as she swam toward Gertie and grabbed hold of the signs.

"What are you doing?" Gertie shouted. "These are Denny's signs. Let go of them, let go of them!"

"Gertie, give them to me!"

"Let go!"

There was a brief struggle but being stuck in the sand greatly hampered Gertie's efforts. Still, her four hands gripped the signs so tightly that it was all Denise could do to pry them loose from her. Then, despite Gertie's screams of protest, Denise lifted the heavy signs and threw them to the side.

"*Noooo!*" Gertie screamed. She started to fight and claw her way out of the sand. Denise reached down to help, but Gertie would have none of it. At last she dug herself out. But instead of throwing her arms around her creator, as Denise had hoped and dreamed, Gertie raced to the signs, dropped to her knees, and threw her arms around *them*.

"These are Denny's," she cried. "She told *me* to carry them!"

"Gertie, I *am* Denny! Gertie?"

But Gertie wasn't listening. Instead, she spoke to the signs. "Perfect signs, beautiful signs." She gently stroked their surfaces. "Did that mean, awful creature scratch you, hmm?"

Another Last Chance

Denise approached her cautiously. "Gertie . . . Gertie, it's me, Denny."

But there was no response as Gertie continued talking to the signs.

"Gertie, please, it's—"

Suddenly Gertie turned on her. "Stay back!" she screamed, pulling the signs closer to protect them.

Denise came to a stop, puzzled and perplexed. "Gertie?"

"I don't know who you are or what you want, but you keep your hands off my signs!"

"Gertie, it's me . . . it's Denny."

"Liar! Denny would never hurt these signs—Denny would never take them away. These are good signs, perfect signs." She began rockung back and forth on her knees, holding the signs like a lost child clinging to a doll.

"Of course they're good," Denise said as she cautiously resumed her approach. "That's why I made them. But look what's written on them, look what they—"

"Stay back!" Gertie warned.

Denise slowed, but she wouldn't stop. "They say you have to quit hurting yourself and to pay attention to me."

"Stay back, I said!"

"But you're so busy carrying *them* and loving *them*, that you don't even hear *me*."

"These are perfect signs, good signs," Gertie repeated.

"I know they're good signs, but you're not obeying them." By now she'd reached Gertie's side.

"Denny told me to carry them!"

"No, I didn't." Gently, carefully, Denise knelt beside her friend. "That was your idea. I just wanted you to obey them. You don't have to carry them."

"But I . . . I love Denny . . . ," she faltered. "I love Denny and, and she wants me to . . ."

"No," Denise gently answered. "All I want is your safety . . . and your friendship."

"But I . . . I have to help."

Again Denise shook her head. "By trying to help, you were cutting me off."

Tears filled Gertie's eyes. "No, that's not true. I love Denny, I didn't mean to—"

"I know . . . ," Denise said, feeling the moisture well up in her own eyes. She tenderly wrapped her arms around Gertie. " . . . I know."

Barely aware of it, Gertie returned the hug. The two of them knelt there for several moments—each giving and returning the other's embrace. Slowly the anger and hurt began to fade. Slowly the love and affection returned.

Finally Denise reached for the signs. "Here," she gently offered. "Let me help you with those. Let me take—"

"No!" Gertie screamed, pulling them back. "These are Denny's signs! Perfect signs! Good signs!"

"But if you'd just—"

With fierce determination, Gertie hoisted the signs over her head and threw them onto her back.

"Gertie, no—"

The poor thing let out an awful groan as the weight crushed her body. But she would not stop. These signs were her life. They had been given to her, and nothing would separate them from her.

"Gertie, please . . ."

There was no answer. Gertie turned and staggered toward the hole in the wall. Every step forced a moan of agony, and every step pushed her deeper and deeper into the sand.

Another Last Chance

"Gertie, please listen to me!"
But Gertie would not listen to Denise. She was too busy serving her.

Chapter Eleven

Fight of Love

Josh was the first to arrive outside the Machine's giant door. He was followed by Bud, Listro Q, and in the distance poor Aristophenix, who, as usual, was bringing up the rear and gasping for breath.

"Come on!" Josh called over his shoulder. "Hurry!"

At last Aristophenix arrived, wheezing out an apology,

**I'm so sorry that I'm tardy,
but we've run so very far.
And we poets are artists,
not Olympic track stars.**

Josh found himself cringing. No matter how many times he'd heard Aristophenix's awful poetry, he still hadn't got used to it. He reached for the door and with a mighty heave tried to pull it open.

It didn't budge, not an inch.

"Wrong, what's?" Listro Q asked.

"It must be locked," Josh said as he tried to pull again with exactly the same results. He turned to Bud. So did the others.

Suddenly Bud remembered. "Oh, the key key, of course." He reached into his coat pocket as he crossed to the keyhole. "Can't get inside without the key key."

But there was nothing in that pocket. So he tried the next . . . "Yes, sir, it always helps to have the key key."

Still nothing.

He tried his pants pockets. "The key key," he muttered.

Then, finally turning to the group, he asked, "By the way, have any of you seen it?"

Fight of Love

They stared at him blankly.

"No, I guess not," he mumbled as he retried each pocket.

"Where last use it did you?" Listro Q asked.

"Why, right here at this door door," Bud insisted. "I unlocked this door door and put the key key someplace where I'd be sure to remember."

"Where was that?" Josh asked, already fearing the worst.

Bud looked at him and shrugged. "I don't remember."

The group groaned.

"Wait a minute!" he shouted. "Of course! I put it someplace safe safe where no one could find it."

"*Where*?" everyone shouted in unison.

"Why, right on the console beside Denny."

The group stared at him in disbelief. Once again he shrugged.

Then, without a word, all four turned and began banging on the door. "Denny! Denny, can you hear us? Denny! Denny, open up!"

But Denise did not answer. Apparently, she couldn't hear.

But the group did. And what they heard brought a look of surprise to all of their faces. It was an electronic sound, one they all recognized . . .

BEEP!........B°P!........BⁱEEP!.......BURP!....

"Gertie, please!" Denise shouted. "You've got to listen to me!"

By now Gertie was dragging herself through the hole in the wall. The bone-crushing weight of the signs took their toll with every step, but she had to get away. Apparently Denise had started to make sense, and that was something Gertie could not allow.

But Denise wouldn't be shaken. She stayed right at her side. "Gertie, please, let *me* carry those . . . please."

Finally they passed through the hole and—

"Hey, Gertie, who's your friend?" Denise looked ahead to see Gus. He was standing right on the edge of their world—teetering back and forth like a tightrope walker in the circus. And beyond him? Beyond him was an awful black void of nothingness—a void that roared and screamed as it smashed into the liquid light—a void as dark and terrifying as the one Denise had experienced on her first trip to Fayrah.

"Gus!" Denise cried, "Get away from there!"

But Gus barely heard. The roar was too loud. Instead, he gave a grin, leaped high into the air, and made a perfect 360-degree spin—well, almost. His right foot slipped and he started to lose his balance.

"*Nooo!*" Denise screamed as she started for him.

But at the last second, Gus caught himself and turned to her, laughing. "Listen, I don't know who you are, but you're gonna have to loosen up a little. Besides, fallin' over the edge is the best part. Come on over here and give it a try."

Denise shook her head and shouted over the roar, "Gus, you've got to listen to me! You're going to—"

But Gus wasn't listening. If she wasn't interested in his little hobby, he'd find somebody who was. "Hey, Gertie!" he called. "You oughta try this."

Gertie just stood, panting—slowly sinking under her heavy burden. "No, thanks," she groaned. "I've got these signs to carry."

"Signs? What for?"

"They're from Denny—to make us happy. She wants us to carry them!"

"No, that's not true!" Denise shouted.

"Happy?" Gus scoffed.

"Yeah!" Gertie shouted. "Carrying them makes you happy!"

Fight of Love

"Right," he laughed. "Looks like you're havin' a terrific time!"

"They're not so bad, once you get used to them." She adjusted the weight and grimaced slightly. "Want to try one?"

"Forget it!" he yelled back. "If you're looking for good times, this is the ticket!"

Gertie gave a doubtful look past him and into the roaring void.

"Don't worry about that," he shouted. "It ain't as scary as it looks."

"I don't know," Gertie answered nervously.

"What's the matter?" he teased. "Chicken?"

"Maybe."

"Come on," he laughed, doing a quick little 180-degree hop. "You won't know till you try. What do you say?"

"Don't listen to him!" Denise shouted. "He doesn't know what he's doing!" There was no hiding her desperation. If Gertie joined Gus on the edge, she could lose them both. "I'm not there any-more!" she shouted. "I can't catch him! I can't catch you!"

"Come on, Gertie!" he called, giving a little hop and a spin on one foot. "Give it a try, it's a real hoot!"

Almost against her will, Gertie was starting to listen.

"And you can bring those signs," he continued. "I mean, if you really think you have to."

"I can?"

"Gertie . . . no!" Denise cried. "Gus, please!"

"Sure," Gus answered as he leaped into the air, landing on all four hands. He did a little jig before hopping back to his feet. "Come on! You gotta try it!"

Gertie readjusted her load. "You're really sure it's safe?"

"Hey, I'm still here, ain't I?"

"Gertie, no!"

Gertie threw Denise a quick glance, then looked back at Gus.

Denise knew exactly what she was thinking. It had been so long since the two of them had played together. Gus had always been fun and he'd never done anything to hurt her. Why would he start now? Besides, she'd worked plenty hard serving Denise by carrying the signs, so she was entitled to a little fun.

"All right!" Gertie finally shouted. "But just for a bit!" She staggered toward him.

"*No!*" Denise screamed. She raced forward and leaped the few feet separating them. She grabbed Gertie and tackled her hard to the ground. The signs fell to the sand as the two rolled back and forth, all four feet kicking, all eight arms flying.

"Let go! Where are my signs!" Gertie screamed. "Let go of me!"

"Listen to me, Gertie, listen to me!"

As they rolled and tumbled in the sand, Gus looked on, laughing.

"Gertie, please—"

"I want my signs!"

"Gertie—"

At last Gertie managed to grab the closest sign. As she pulled it to herself, Denise tried to break her grip. "Gertie . . ."

"My sign . . ."

"Gertie, let me have it . . ."

Finally, rolling onto her back, Gertie tucked her legs into her chest and kicked out. Her feet landed squarely in Denise's stomach, throwing her backward with an *ooaaaf!*

But Denise was determined. Catching her breath and crawling onto her hands and knees, she gasped, "Gertie . . . please!"

Gertie was already reaching for the other sign.

Denise staggered to her feet and lunged again.

But this time Gertie had a weapon. Raising the sign high over her shoulder, she leaned back like a batter waiting to hit a ball.

Fight of Love

Denise saw what was about to happen and tried to stop. But the momentum in the liquid light kept her moving forward until suddenly, *swooosh*, Gertie took a swing. The steel sliced through the liquid. Its sharp corner caught Denise hard, ripping through her clothing, cutting into her side.

At first all Denise noticed was the look of shock on Gertie's face. She glanced down and saw blood clouding the liquid around them. Next she saw the gash in her side—deep and ugly. Finally she felt the pain. Sharp, searing, relentless. She slowly raised her eyes from the bleeding wound and looked back at Gertie.

No one said a word. Everything was silent as the liquid light grew more and more cloudy.

Denise tried to breathe, but each breath sent the burning, jagged pain deeper into her body. Slowly the edges around her vision started to grow white and blur. Her legs turned weak and rubbery, but only for a second. Then, they gave out altogether and she crumpled to the ground.

"Ha!" Gus laughed. "Serves her right!"

Gertie continued to stare, horrified at what she had done—unsure what she should do . . . as the liquid light grew darker and darker . . .

Chapter Twelve

Reunion

"Aristophenix! Listro Q!"

The group spun around to see Josh's little brother, Nathan. He had just popped in with his stuffed English bulldog, Mr. Hornsberry. Oh, and they had one other companion—Samson, the half dragonfly, half ladybug who had become such good friends with Denise on their last journey together.

"Nathan!" Josh cried. "What are you doing here?"

"Samson says Denny's in some sort of trouble."

"But how'd you get here?"

Nathan held up another Cross-Dimensionalizer exactly like Listro Q's. "It's Samson's. He let me try it out. How'd I do?"

"Good, pretty," Listro Q answered half-grudgingly. Then under his breath he added, "Maybe lessons give me should he."

Samson interrupted with a high squeal question.

Aristophenix answered,

**Denny's in there,
dying for love.
But we're all out here,
'cause the door we can't budge.**

Again Samson chattered.

Bud answered, "The fault is mine. I left the key key inside."

For a moment the group was unsure what to do. That is until Mr. Hornsberry cleared his throat and spoke up. "Although no one is seeking my advice, would it not be advantageous for us to utilize all of our man and dog power?"

Reunion

"So how?" Listro Q asked.

"My good man," Mr. Hornsberry answered in his usual why-am-I-surrounded-by-morons tone of voice, "all one need do is remove the door from its hinges."

As much as everybody hated to admit it, Mr. Hornsberry had a point. Now there was just the detail of how to do it. It was so tall and huge. Unfortunately everyone had their own opinion and no one was afraid to voice it. Suddenly the air was full of a hundred "if you ask me's . . . ," "we should try's . . . ," and the ever popular, "I'm telling you, my way is better."

On and on they argued as if each was an expert door remover. Of course none of them were, so nothing happened—except more arguing—until, finally, ever so slowly, the door began to swing open by itself.

"What on earth," someone gasped.

"How do you suppose?" another asked.

Then they saw the reason: while everybody was voicing their opinion, Samson simply flew in through the keyhole, unlatched the door from the inside, and with considerable effort, pushed it open.

"All right, Sammy!" everyone cheered as they poured into the laboratory. But the celebration was short-lived.

"Denny!" Josh shouted. "Denny, where are you?"

The others joined in, calling her name. "Denny? Denny!"

But there was no answer. She was nowhere to be found.

Josh turned to Bud. "What's going on?" he asked.

"I don't know know," Bud said as they approached the deserted platform of sand and light. "Denny!" he called. "Denny!"

Still no answer. "You must know something!" Josh demanded.

Bud gave no reply. Instead, he turned to the platform and ordered, "Machine!"

The Machine hummed louder.

"Where is Denny?"

With a faint crackle the monitor above the platform flickered. Everyone gasped as the image of Denise appeared—not because of her four arms or because she was lying unconscious in the liquid light. They gasped because of the bleeding wound in her side.

"*Denny!*" Josh called. "*Denise!*"

"She can't hear you you," Bud said.

"Listen to me!" Josh turned his anger on Bud. "You got her into this mess, now you get her out!"

"I . . . can't!" Bud stammered. "This was her decision, this was her—"

Josh grabbed the little man by his lab coat and pulled him directly into his face. "I don't care whose decision it was!" he shouted. "Do what you have to do to save her!"

"But . . . bu—"

"*Now!*"

"The only way to save her is to to reduce someone to her size size and rescue her."

"Do it!" Josh shouted.

"But you don't understand how dangerous it is. It could—"

"Then do it to me!"

"But—"

"Do it to me, *now!*" Joshua glared at him, making it clear that he didn't have a choice.

Finally Bud nodded. "Machine Machine," he called.

The Machine crackled in response.

"Take Joshua here and—"

UNTIL ALL IS ACCOMPLISHED
DO NOT INTERFERE.

Reunion

The voice stunned Josh. But it wasn't a voice. It was a thought that vibrated inside his head. He spun around to the rest of the group. By their expressions it was obvious it had vibrated in all of their heads.

"What . . . who was that?" he whispered.

At first, no one answered. Then, with a nervous swallow, Bud spoke, "Imager."

Everyone remained silent. Even Mr. Hornsberry. It was the strongest, most commanding voice Josh had ever heard. And yet, at the same time, it was the gentlest and most soothing.

Then he heard another. "Please . . ."

It was Denise!

His eyes shot up to the monitor. She had regained consciousness and was dragging her bleeding body toward two other creatures with multiple arms. One stood on the very edge of the platform; the other was being crushed by two large rectangular plates of steel on its back.

"Gertie," Denise gasped. "Gus . . ."

But the creatures did not answer.

Instead, the bigger one turned to the smaller one. "Hit her!" he shouted. "Hit her again!"

The smaller one hesitated.

Denise continued to approach. "Gertie . . ."

"Hit her!" the bigger one cried. "You have to stop her! She won't quit unless you stop her!"

Again the smaller one hesitated.

"Hit her! Hit her! Hit her!"

Reluctantly, the smaller one raised the steel plates high overhead and brought them down hard onto Denise's back.

Everyone in the lab cried out as the blow smashed her to the ground.

And yet, Denise wouldn't stop. She slowly rose to her hands and knees and continued toward them. "Please . . . ," she groaned.

Once again the smaller creature raised the plates and once again she slammed them hard into Denise's back.

Josh could take no more. That was his friend up there on the screen and, Imager or not, he wasn't going to stand and watch her beaten to death. He shouted at the thought or the voice or whatever it was inside his head. "What type of logic is this?"

There was no response, only silence—and a few nervous coughs among the group.

"Answer me!"

More silence.

"You claim to be so logical . . . so loving, then answer me! Answer me!"

Finally the voice spoke. But it wasn't angry. It was tender and understanding. Yet it was also firm—very firm.

UNTIL ALL IS ACCOMPLISHED
DO NOT INTERFERE.

"But she's dying!" Josh shouted. "She's killing herself! Where's the logic in that? Answer me! *Answer me!*"

The response rang loud and clear . . . and very, very gentle.

UNTIL ALL IS ACCOMPLISHED
DO NOT INTERFERE.

"Until what is accomplished? How will we know? What can we do?"

There was no answer.

Josh repeated, "*How will we know?*"

Reunion

But the voice did not answer. Apparently it had said all that it intended to say. Now there was only silence.

Josh sighed loudly and turned to the others. Everyone looked equally baffled and confused. Everyone but Samson.

The little fellow flew closer to the platform and seemed to be waiting. Denise had often told Josh how close she and the little bug had become. How, of all the creatures in Fayrah, their personalities seemed the most similar. And, although the little guy said nothing, Josh could tell he was thinking.

But for now there was nothing they could do. Imager had spoken . . . three times he had spoken. Now they could only watch and obey. . . .

◙

As Gertie continued clutching the signs, their weight continued to force her deeper and deeper into the sand. But that was nothing compared to Denise's pain. Again and again, Gertie had to strike her, and again and again, Denise rose and continued toward them. Nothing would stop her. Not the gaping wound in her side that continued darkening the liquid, and not the brutal beating of the signs. Granted, each time Denise rose, she rose a little slower, but she rose, nonetheless. She had to in order to save her friends.

Soon she had backed them up to the edge of the platform, just inches from the roaring black emptiness. "Please . . . ," she gasped hoarsely. "Please . . ."

"What do you want?" Gertie screamed. "What do you want from us?!"

"I want you to live . . ."

"You're crazy!" Gus shouted. "We *are* living!"

Denise shook her head and with great effort reached for the signs. "Please . . ."

"You're holding back!" Gus shouted at Gertie over the roaring void. "Stop holding back and hit her with everything you got! Make it hurt so much that she'll never bother us again!"

Denise looked up. She could see Gertie didn't like this, not one bit. The poor little thing was already crying over the pain she'd inflicted. Still, the look in her eyes said that she believed something had to be done.

"Go ahead," Gus demanded. "Everything you got!"

Gertie took a trembling breath.

"Don't hold back!"

Another breath.

"If you don't, she'll never give us rest. Go ahead! *Go ahead*!"

Finally, Gertie lifted the signs high over her head. She leaned back, closed her eyes, and—

"*No!*" Another voice shouted. Denise recognized it instantly.

"Who are you?" Gus shouted.

"She's our friend," Gertie answered. "The one who taught us about free will."

"Don't listen to her," Denise croaked, reaching up and clinging to Gertie's sleeve. "She's the Illusionist . . . she'll kill—"

"Destroy her!" the Illusionist shrieked.

"What?" Gus asked, obviously surprised at the outburst.

The Illusionist cleared her throat and regained control. "It's only a suggestion—after all, I don't want to interfere with your free will. But if you ask me, hitting her is not enough. You must completely destroy her by throwing her off the edge."

"But she'll come back," Gus explained. "*I* always have."

The Illusionist grinned. "Trust me, she won't come back—not this time."

"But . . . why?" Gertie asked, obviously confused. "Why do we have to destroy her?"

Reunion

"It's for her own good," the Illusionist cooed. "It's the kindest thing to do, dear heart. Otherwise she'll just keep coming at you and you'll just have to keep hurting her."

Moved with pity, Gertie looked down at Denise.

The Illusionist continued. "You've inflicted such pain upon her already. But no matter how much she bleeds, no matter how often you strike her, she does not give up."

Gertie nodded sadly.

"It deeply grieves me"—the Illusionist pretended to have a catch in her throat—"but the only way you can stop her, the only way you can put her out of her misery, is to completely destroy her."

Then, turning to Gus, the Illusionist used an entirely different approach. "The wretched thing has no pride," she hissed. "If you don't destroy her, she'll always create problems. Just look at the way her blood is darkening your perfect ocean, just listen to the way she's nagging and begging. She'll never give you rest."

Denise watched Gus, hoping he'd see the lie.

"Do it!" the Illusionist cried. Then, turning to Gertie, she resumed her more gentle approach. "You can keep those perfect signs forever and ever." Then, turning back to Gus, she added with a sneer, "And you can jump off that edge anytime you want. No one will stop you. No one will stop either of you!"

"No one?" they asked in unison.

"Certainly not me." The Illusionist grinned. "I wouldn't dream of stopping you!"

The two glanced at each other, then down at Denise.

She no longer had the strength to speak. She could only shake her head, her eyes pleading with them.

The Illusionist stifled a yawn. "When you stop to think about it, you really have no other choice."

Gus was the first to agree. He began nodding his head and turned to Gertie. "Grab her arms," he ordered.

"There's no other way?" Gertie asked, her little voice filled with sorrow.

"You heard her, didn't you?"

Gertie nodded. Slowly she stooped down to Denise. "I'm sorry," she gently whispered, "but this really is for your best."

Denise shook her head violently, but Gertie would not listen. Instead, holding her signs high above with one pair of hands, Gertie tenderly took Denise's face with her other pair. "Maybe . . . maybe if you'd stop trying to help us—maybe, if you'd just let us have our way instead of always—"

Denise shook her head. She opened her mouth to explain, but could not speak.

Slowly, sadly Gertie rose to her feet. "I'm sorry," she repeated, tears streaming down her cheeks. "I'm so sorry." Then, taking Denise's arms with her two free hands, she gently raised her off the ground.

Denise clenched her eyes shut. The pain was too great. But it was not the pain of her wounds, or even the thought of being destroyed. It was the pain of a breaking heart.

Gus picked up her feet. Now she was suspended between the two of them.

"On the count of three," Gus ordered.

Gertie nodded.

"One." They swung her out over the edge and back.

"Two." They swung her further out and back.

"Three . . ."

But at the last second, using what little strength she had, Denise lunged for the signs in Gertie's other hands. She latched onto them as she swung out the third and final time. And, as she did, the momentum ripped them from Gertie's grasp.

Before they could catch her, Denise slipped from their hands and started to fall.

"My signs!" Gertie cried as Denise and the signs tumbled into the roaring darkness. "My beautiful signs!"

Chapter Thirteen

To the Rescue

The group inside the Machine cried out as Denise fell.

Everyone but Samson.

While the others had been staring at the monitor over their heads, Samson had hovered near the platform carefully searching the liquid light. He had spotted Gus and Gertie's location by the slight ripples near the edge. And, as soon as Denise began to fall, he made his move.

"Samson!" Nathan shouted. "What are you—"

But there was no time to explain. Imager had said, "Until all is accomplished." Well, as far as Samson could tell *all* had been accomplished. Now the little guy couldn't waste a second.

He swooped toward the platform's edge. And just as Denise had done so many times with Gus, Samson managed to spot the tiny pinpoint glimmer of her reflection. He raced toward it for all he was worth.

Faster and faster she fell.

Swifter and swifter he flew. He saw the approaching floor, but it didn't matter. He moved into position. Quickly he swooped under her. For the briefest instant he felt her hit his back. But they were traveling too fast. Although she landed, her speed forced her to tumble across him until she shot off the other side . . . and continued to fall.

Samson spun around and dove after her again.

But the floor was much closer. Much, much closer.

Common sense told him to pull out of the dive before it was too late. If he didn't, they'd both smash into the floor. *It's better to*

To the Rescue

lose one life than two. That's what his mind said. But Samson's heart was bigger than his mind.

He folded back his wings and dove even faster.

The floor raced toward him.

Now he was even with Denise. In just another second he would be able to swoop underneath and let her land on his back again. Unfortunately, they didn't have another second.

In desperation, Samson unfolded his right wing and thrust it into the roaring wind toward Denise. The air screamed and tugged at the wing, nearly ripping it out of its socket. But Samson endured the pain and continued to stretch his wing until it was finally beneath her.

Then he felt it—Denise's tiny presence landing on him. In a flash, he reversed course, using only one wing, buzzing twice as hard, struggling to navigate, until he was finally able to pull up. It was close. So close that he actually felt the lab's floor brush his hind legs as he zoomed away. But he made it. As he rose, he lifted his right wing until Denise rolled down it and onto his back. Now, he could use both wings. And now, at last, she was safe.

For Denise it had been quite a landing. She'd had the breath knocked out of her, but she didn't complain. She was just grateful to have breath to be knocked out! She was so tiny that she had no idea what she'd landed upon. As far as she knew it was some sort of elevator that was quickly shooting upward. Still, who had ever heard of an elevator with a gauzy, semitransparent floor . . . and a huge flickering taillight in the back?

But Denise had little time to wonder, for suddenly the platform came back into view. And there, standing on its edge, were Gus and Gertie—both staring out at her in amazement. On the wall behind them, the Illusionist was jumping up and down screaming, "Unfair! Unfair! Unfair!"

For a moment the "elevator" slowed and drew nearer to the edge. Gus and Gertie came so close that Denise could have reached out and touched them . . . if she'd had the strength.

"Unfair!" the Illusionist continued to scream. "Unfair! Unfair!" But no one paid attention.

"I'll be back," Denise called. She was so weak her voice was only a whisper—barely audible over the roaring void. Still, somehow they seemed to understand. Gertie was the first to nod. Then slowly, almost reluctantly, Gus joined in. And then . . . was it just her imagination, or had the slightest trace of a smile started to cross their faces?

The elevator began to rise up and away. Faster and faster it rose. Soon Gus and Gertie shrank to tiny dots, and then to nothing at all.

But in her mind, Denise still saw them. She suspected she would always see them. "I'll be back," she whispered again. "I promise, I'll be back . . ."

▣

For the next several days, Denise did little but eat and sleep. Once the Machine had transformed her to normal size, the group had whisked her out of the lab and off to Samson's home in Fayrah—well, at least to a huge tent they had erected beside his home. (Humans are a bit large for insect homes—especially newlywed insects just starting out.) Here she would rest until she was strong enough to return to the Upside-Down Kingdom. According to the doctor, her mind and body had been through a great trauma, and they needed time to heal.

"But what about Mom? What about Josh's grandpa?" Denise protested. "They'll be worried sick."

To the Rescue

"Worry, don't you," Listro Q assured her.

Aristophenix agreed. "Remember,

> **We're running in time,**
> **much faster than you reckon.**
> **For us, what's a week,**
> **to them's but a second.**

"Right is he," Listro Q agreed. "Teapot remember in Grandpa's shop that dropped you?"

"The one that floated?"

Listro Q nodded. "Floating, still is it."

Denise looked at him in wonder. But before she could say anything, Violet, Samson's new bride, buzzed in and began chattering a mile a second.

"What's she saying?" Denise asked.

Aristophenix gave a hasty explanation,

> **She's saying yer her guest,**
> **and that there isn't a doubt,**
> **you'll be getting some rest,**
> **'cause . . . well . . . she's throwing us out!**

Denise couldn't hold back a giggle as she watched Violet buzz and dive-bomb the guests standing inside her tent.

"All right, we're going, we're going!" they shouted, raising their arms and stumbling toward the exit. "Come on, Vi, give us a break. Samson, will you call her off!"

But Samson didn't call her off. And Violet didn't stop until every one of them was out of the tent.

"That's quite a wife you have," Denise said, grinning over at Samson.

Samson chattered back a proud reply but was cut short as he, too, was shooed out of the tent.

Six more days passed before the doctor finally gave Denise permission to travel. And once word spread that they were going, Samson's yard was filled with hundreds of well-wishers and bon-voyagers. Some of them had never even met Denise, but they'd all heard of her deeds.

"Now you take care of this side," the doctor warned as he changed the dressing and bandages on her wound for the last time. "It'll be a while before it's completely healed."

Denise nodded.

"And I'm afraid you'll always have a scar," he added. "Quite a large one."

Denise looked down at the red, jagged line that ran from the middle of her ribs all the way to her hip. "That's okay," she said quietly. "It'll help me remember." Then, before she knew it, tears filled her eyes and began to fall . . . just as they had so many times throughout the week.

"Thinking about Gus and Gertie again?" Josh asked quietly.

She gave a quick nod and tried to brush the tears away. "And Imager too," she mumbled. Looking up she spotted Aristophenix and Listro Q standing nearby. She continued softly, "He really does care for us, doesn't he?"

They nodded in silence.

"I mean, if he only feels a fraction of what I felt for Gus and Gertie . . ." Her voice trailed off.

"More," Listro Q gently added, "more many times . . . for us each does he."

Denise could only shake her head in amazement. "How can he stand it?" she whispered hoarsely. "The joy . . . the pain . . ." Barely

To the Rescue

aware, she reached up and touched the scar in her side, remembering. "How can he stand it?"

For a long moment, everyone stood in silence. Until, suddenly—

"Step back, please . . . coming through, yes, we are. Stand back!" The silence was shattered by the Weaver's entrance. Following behind him were two of his assistants, each carrying an easel and small tapestry. Behind them several of the folks who had been patiently waiting in the yard squeezed in. Before Denise knew it, her tent was packed so tightly that no amount of buzzing and dive-bombing by Violet could unpack it.

"Oh, there you are!" The Weaver shouted to Denise above the noise. "Getting better are we?"

She nodded.

"Good!" he said. Then, turning back to his assistants he called, "Just set those up anywhere, boys."

"What are you doing here?" Denise asked.

"Rumor has it you're concerned about Gus and Gertie, yes, you are. Well, no need to be. I brought their tapestries along to show you before you go."

"Gus and Gertie have tapestries?" Denise asked in astonishment.

"Of course! You don't think I'd let something like that slip by, do you?"

"Well, no, I guess . . ."

The assistants had placed the veiled tapestries up on their easels. The Weaver gave a nod and, with a dramatic flair, they removed the covers.

The crowd gasped, then broke into applause.

The Weaver grinned and nodded politely. Then, turning to Denise, he asked, "So what do you think?"

Denise could only stare. They were more beautiful than she could have imagined. Each thread shimmered and danced with light—each design, down to the tiniest detail, perfectly captured their personalities. In fact, the patterns were so perfect that as she stared she could practically see and hear Gus and Gertie again. Unfortunately this only brought on another grimace of pain and more tears.

"Come now, they're not that ugly," the Weaver protested.

Denise shook her head. "No, they were beautiful . . . wonderful."

"What do you mean *were*? As you can see by their length both Gus and Gertie will be living for many more epochs."

"They're still alive?" Denise cried.

"Well, yes, of course," the Weaver said. "As are their children and their children's children and their—"

"They have children too?!"

Again the Weaver tried to overlook her interruption. "Of course, thousands of them. And according to this thread here—"

"They have thousands of children?!"

"If you keep interrupting," the Weaver said evenly, "we won't get through this before you leave."

Denise nodded and did her best to remain silent, though her mind reeled with excitement. She'd just naturally thought that Gus had talked Gertie into jumping off the edge with him. But the fact that they were still alive and that they actually had children, well, the possibility had Denise so excited that she could barely sit still.

"Now where was I?" the Weaver asked. "Oh, yes. This thread here"—he pointed to the first tapestry—"indicates Gus's continual fascination with the edge. But, instead of leaping off, he has taken Gertie's advice and has devoted his life to studying it."

"Studying it?" Denise asked.

To the Rescue

"Yes, *scientific evaluation* I believe they call it."

"Gus has become a scientist?"

"Yes, well, I'm afraid Bud has taken over leadership while you were away, and has had some impact upon—"

"Oh, no," Josh groaned. "Bud is their leader?"

Denise giggled. "I hope he doesn't drop anything on them."

Others in the tent also chuckled. Apparently Bud's reputation for grace was known far and wide.

The Weaver resumed, "And just as Gus has continued his scientific studies, Gertie has been writing and teaching her children poetry."

Denise kept listening, hanging on to every word. The news was so good. So very, very good.

"And do you see this scarlet thread here?" the Weaver asked, turning to the group, while pointing to a deep red thread. "This is most intriguing. See how it runs through the center of both patterns, seeming to hold them together?"

Everyone in the tent nodded.

He turned directly to Denise. "That thread is you, my girl, yes, it is. *You* are what they speak of in science class. *You* are what they write about in their poetry."

Suddenly Denise broke into laughter . . . and more tears.

"Good gracious, *now* what is it?" the Weaver demanded.

"I'm sorry," Denise said sheepishly while drying her eyes. "It's just . . . well, the thing is . . ." She tried to explain but couldn't. Everything was just too good. Too perfect. And that meant laughter . . . and more tears.

But it wasn't only Denise. It seemed everyone in the tent had suddenly come down with a good case of smiles and sniffles . . . everyone but Mr. Hornsberry. Stuffed dogs know better than to cry—they mildew.

"I say there," the animal said, clearing his throat in his usual snooty manner. "What about that dreadful Illusionist creature? Where is she in their tapestries?"

"Right here," the Weaver said, pointing to a dark, ominous thread. "As you can see, she makes an appearance from time to time, but her effect upon the overall work is minimal at best, yes, it is."

The Weaver pointed back at the scarlet thread. "But Denise's thread not only keeps appearing in their tapestries, but in their children's, and in their children's children. They will remember her life throughout their existence . . . passing her exploits down from one generation to the next. In fact, until the end of time, they will insist she is the one responsible for the subtle rose hue that colors their ocean. They will say this is to remind them of her love as well as her promise to return. A promise"—he turned to Denise—"that as their creator, you are bound to keep."

Denise nodded eagerly. There would be no problem keeping that promise. In fact, she wouldn't mind keeping it right now. But that was out of the question. For now, at least, she would have to return home.

"That's all I have to say," the Weaver concluded. "You better get a move on, yes, you better. If I remember your patterns correctly, you'll be leaving here"—he glanced at his watch—"in less than forty-eight seconds."

The tent exploded into action. Everyone began hugging, shouting thank-yous, saying goodbyes, and making the usual promises to stay in touch.

It was during this confusion that Josh pulled the Weaver aside. "Listen," he said. "I just want to thank you. I mean, I know I was a bit of a pain, not believing and everything."

To the Rescue

"Most of you are," the Weaver chuckled. "But we're getting used to it."

Josh smiled and continued, "If you could also tell Bud thanks for me—I mean, I didn't get to say much when we rushed Denny out of there and everything. But he really did help me . . . a lot."

"You'll get a chance to thank him yourself," the Weaver answered. "Yes, you will."

"What?" Josh asked. "When?"

The Weaver lowered his voice and glanced about the room to make sure he wasn't overheard. "I shouldn't say anything, but in several months he will be cross-dimensionalizing over to your world."

"That's great!" Josh exclaimed.

The Weaver scowled slightly. "Perhaps. But the reason will be most urgent."

"But everything will be okay?" Josh asked. "I mean, everything will be all right?"

The Weaver took a deep breath. For a moment it looked like he would answer, then suddenly he changed his mind. "I've said too much already."

"Oh, come on!" Josh pleaded.

"Josh, go let's!" Listro Q called. He had grouped all those heading back to the Upside-Down Kingdom at the far end of the tent.

But Josh paid little attention. He was still searching the Weaver's face. "You've got to tell me *something*."

"Just . . . be careful. It will be a most critical time, yes it will."

"But we'll be all right," Josh insisted. "Won't we?"

"Go let's. Come on, Josh . . ."

The group started pulling him away, leading him toward Listro Q. With a few more tugs and jostles, they finally placed him alongside Denise, Nathan, Mr. Hornsberry, Aristophenix, and Listro

Q. Josh searched the crowd for the Weaver, but he had already disappeared.

"Alrightie!" Aristophenix shouted.

> **Let's move, let's go;**
> **let's have no more stops.**
> **It's straight from Fayrah,**
> **to Grandpa's Secondhand Shop.**

"Good-bye," everyone shouted. "See you later . . . bye-bye . . ." Denise caught Violet's and Samson's eyes. It was too noisy to be heard, so she could only mouth the words. "Thank you," she said.

Both insects understood and flickered their red taillights in response.

Listro reached for his Cross-Dimensionalizer and prepared to punch in the coordinates.

"Need any help with that?" Nathan teased.

"Manage think can I," Listro Q grinned back. Then he pushed the four buttons.

BEEP!........BOP!........BLEEP!.......BURP!....

Suddenly the group was crossing through the Center with all of its glory and splendor. And, although there was plenty more to see, they knew that it would have to wait for another time. They would return again. And when they did they knew they would not be disappointed. Unfortunately, at that moment, they should have also known something else. Listro Q's aim—

CRASH, BANG, CLATTER, TINKLE-TINKLE-TINKLE . . .

To the Rescue

—had not improved.

This time he only missed their landing coordinates by a few feet. But inside Grandpa O'Brien's cluttered shop, a few feet was as good as a mile.

"Listro Q . . . ," Aristophenix cried.

"Cool, is it," came the reply.

And so, with the appropriate groans and complaints, everyone climbed out of the front window's display of pots and pans. For some it was quite a struggle. "It's stuck to my rear," Aristophenix cried. "Will someone please pull this thing off my rear?" But no one fussed too much. After all, practice makes perfect. And over the course of time, Listro Q would have many more opportunities to get his coordinates right for traveling into that shop.

Many, many more . . .

About the Author

Bill Myers is the author of the humorously imaginative *The Incredible Worlds of Wally McDoogle* series. Bill's latest works include the creation of a brand new secret agent series for early readers, *Secret Agent Dingledorf.* He is also the creator and writer of the *McGee & Me!* video series. Bill is a director as well as a writer, and his films have won over forty national and international awards. He has written more than 50 books for kids, teens, and adults. Bill lives with his wife and two daughters in Southern California.

You'll want to read them all!

The Imager Chronicles

*Who knew that the old rock found forgotten in an attic
was actually the key to a fantastic alternate world?*

When Denise, Nathan, and Joshua stumble into the land of
Fayrah, ruled by the Imager—the One who makes us in His
image—they are drawn into wonderful adventures that teach them
about life, faith, and the all-encompassing heart of God.

BOOK ONE: THE PORTAL

Denise and Nathan meet a myriad of interesting characters in
the wondrous world they've discovered, but soon Nathan's selfish
nature—coupled with some tricky moves by the evil Illusionist—
gets him imprisoned. Denise and her new friends try desperately
to free Nathan from the villain, but one of them must make an
enormous sacrifice—or they will all be held captive!

BOOK THREE: THE WHIRLWIND

Once again the mysterious stone transports the three friends to Fayrah, where they find themselves caught between good and evil. When Josh falls under the spell of the trickster Illusionist and his henchman Bobok—who convince him that he can become perfect—Denise and Nathan must enlist the help of Someone who is truly perfect before they lose Josh in the Sea of Justice. Will help come in time?

BOOK FOUR: THE TABLET

When Denise finds a tablet with mysterious powers, she is beguiled by the chance to fulfill her own desires—instead of trusting the Imager's plan. When Josh and Nathan grasp the danger she faces, they work desperately to stop the Merchant of Emotions before he destroys Denise—and the whole world!